Loyal Stalkers

AF632166

Also by Chhimi Tenduf-La

The Amazing Racist
Panther

Loyal Stalkers

Chhimi Tenduf-La

MACMILLAN

First published 2017 by Macmillan
an imprint of Pan Macmillan India
a division of Macmillan Publishers India Private Limited
707, Kailash Building
26, K. G. Marg, New Delhi 110001
www.panmacmillan.co.in

Pan Macmillan, the Smithson, 6 Briset St, London EC1M 5NR, United Kingdom
Basingstoke and Oxford
Associated companies throughout the world
www.panmacmillan.com

ISBN 978-93-82616-92-4

Copyright © Chhimi Tenduf-La 2017

'White Knight' appeared in an earlier form in *Panther*, published by
HarperCollins India 2015

This is a work of fiction. All characters, locations and events are fictitious.
Any resemblance to actual events or locales or persons, living or dead,
is entirely coincidental.

All rights reserved. No part of this publication may be reproduced, stored in or introduced into a retrieval system, or transmitted, in any form, or by any means (electronic, mechanical, photocopying, recording or otherwise) without the prior written permission of the publisher. Any person who does any unauthorized act in relation to this publication may be liable to criminal prosecution and civil claims for damages.

3 5 7 9 8 6 4

This book is sold subject to the condition that it shall not, by way of trade or otherwise, be lent, re-sold, hired out, or otherwise circulated without the publisher's prior consent in any form of binding or cover other than that in which it is published and without a similar condition including this condition being imposed on the subsequent purchaser.

Typeset by R Ajith Kumar, New Delhi
Printed and bound in India by Repro India Ltd

To Sam, Tara Mae and Jetty Boy

Contents

Sending a Night Breeze 1
Pot Holiness 11
White Knight 23
Lovable Idiot 39
Devil Mask Tattoo 57
Tuk Tuk Bang 67
My Fair & Lovely Lady 77
Old Boys' Nuts 87
Loyal Stalker 105
The Dog Thrown off a Building 143
Everyone Has to Eat 153
Help, Help 167
Suspiciously Brown 183
Graveyard Tail 203
Balls 215
Acknowledgements 231

Sending a Night Breeze

He wears swimming goggles and a bright yellow raincoat.

I am naked from the waist down.

He scratches his bald head and leans over me. No love in his eyes. No hate. No warmth. Nothing. As if he has never seen me before.

He tightens the straps on his goggles and sits in a rocking chair, while the fourteen-year-old maid pulls up his Wellington boots.

I am drugged up to my eyeballs. As far as I can remember, this is the first time I am not scared of him. Instead, I love him even though he has never coveted my affection.

He is my father.

The maid lifts one of my legs. The eighty-year-old nurse, chosen because she has no memory, raises the other.

It is July 1983 and there are riots and curfews in Colombo. This barely registers with our family, because I am seventeen years old, unmarried, and having a baby.

My father delivers babies for a living, most of the time in a hospital. For a hefty fee, he also performs unrecorded deliveries to spare the shame of anyone in Sri Lanka whose lives are ruled by what their neighbours think. When he does these home deliveries, he is careful that blood does not get onto his person or in his eyes. The goggles, I have always been convinced, are more for effect than necessity, to intimidate in a way he thinks is mischievous rather than cruel. Like how, as a diabetic, he sits at the dining table and injects his stomach in front of us while we're eating. A smile on his face – and this is a man who rarely shows any joy. Not to his wife and daughter anyway.

I am charged a nominal fee for this delivery, because I am family. My mother insists I pay something even though I could have had it done for free at a government hospital.

'But what is the price for being judged?' she asks me. 'What is the price of shame?'

She is not here, but that's no surprise. I cannot remember her ever hugging or kissing me. I'm told she never rocked me to sleep as a baby, burped me, consoled me. Those kind of things were left to the youngest maid she had in her employment. Still, I always imagined her holding my hand when I was giving birth. I imagined holding a hand bigger than mine, but now I am squeezing the small right hand of the fourteen-year-old maid.

My father, your grandfather, looks at me. He could be a gym instructor. A drill sergeant. 'Push, duwa, when I tell you.'

'Call me sudu duwa, like you normally do,' I say. Technically 'sudu duwa' means white daughter, but I am not all that fair. Maybe it is what they wanted of me. Maybe, since they think it is a good thing to not be dark, my father called me that as a term of affection.

'Push, duwa,' he says. 'Don't waste the contractions.'

As I scream, my mother pokes her head through the door. 'Keep it down.'

I push and push until I cannot open my eyes but when I do, you are in the eighty-year-old nurse's arms. Cleaned, but not clean. My mother nowhere to be seen. My father's spotless raincoat, boots and goggles strewn on the red cement floor.

The fourteen-year-old maid has tears in her eyes. She touches my forehead and it feels nice.

Now you are on my chest. Feeding.

My sudu putha.

It doesn't feel real because it is so familiar. So like I knew it would be, for some reason.

This is love.

You have been assigned a fake surname on your birth certificate, but I am allowed to give you a first name. I am not sure if this is the one act of compassion my mother could muster, or if she could not be bothered to research the numerology herself.

I name you Sidhara.

In numerology the name has the birth path 6 and its meaning is connected to self-confidence and excellence.

Your life purpose will be to reconcile your ideals with reality, and to accept the world as it is. As if you ever had a choice.

My father's always been too busy being pampered by younger nurses to notice babies. He delivers them like he would a package for DHL. But my mother? I want her to see you, perhaps then she will change her mind. I know she cannot show affection. I know she hates to touch or hold or kiss. But she loves me. She loves you. She has a heart.

More importantly to her, she has fair skin, a Kandyan name, money, marriage to a doctor, kids. She has respect and she creates fear for people who have none of these things. No way could she have a seventeen-year-old unmarried daughter with a baby. No way could that baby be given a Kandyan name.

It doesn't make a difference that I was raped. It is still my shame. Still the family's shame.

We keep you for two months. Enough time for me to breastfeed. Enough time, my mother says, for me to get back into shape so I can be seen again. So I can get ready for my official return from the UK where she claims I have been when I was actually hiding my bump.

A Buddhist monk arrives by trishaw. He has no creases in his robes and I wonder how a man living a simple life irons his clothes. That is a distraction. Me conning myself. I know why he is here.

I scream and say, 'If they take him, I will tell the whole of Colombo the truth. I will tell them I had a baby and you gave him away. I will tell them who the father is.'

And I feel the cold edge of a kitchen knife to my throat. My own mother with a blade to my neck, her hand shaking with rage, spit dribbling from her mouth. 'You will do no such thing.'

She smiles to remind me that I do not have the power to upset her. She drops the knife to the floor. That damn knife I hate, its rusted blade ten years past its life expectancy. The knife I was fined for breaking even though it cost twenty-eight rupees new and fifty-six rupees to mend.

Upal and Tharanga drag me away. They need their jobs. I am locked in the upstairs bathroom, standing on the faded green bidet and looking through the gaps in the window frame where the wood has warped. I see the fourteen-year-old maid breaking down on the front lawn. Crying for me. Crying for herself. I don't even know her name.

My father hands you to the monk. I pound at the window, and my hands bleed when the pane cracks. The Buddhist monk looks up at me, with you in his arms. And he smiles. That's all he does. Maybe he means to comfort me. Maybe he means to say everything will be okay because they will look after you like the infant Dalai Lama. Yet, it feels as if he is mocking me. There is no air in this bathroom, I am sure. My legs want to give way but I hang on to watch you as if there's a movie playing on our neighbour's TV.

But just like that, the monk is gone, vanished into a cloud of exhaust fumes from the tuktuk. I can hear you cough, even though you must be too far away for the sound to carry. Because I am your mother.

I will never forget that.

I will never forget you.

I try to kill myself for the first time, but I am stopped. I will try again and again and again until they bring you to me. That is the only leverage I have. The only way to force my parents' hands. The only way to punish them. If it doesn't work, I will continue to kill myself throughout my afterlife until my blood rains down on my parents in front of their neighbours, cousins, aunties and uncles. Then let them all point and whisper.

I am in a Negombo boarding house because my mother knows she can't trust me in Colombo. She knows I will say the wrong thing so she tells everyone I have gone back to the UK. When she visits me, I can see the guilt in her eyes, but I do nothing to make her feel better. Every time she comes, I cry when she opens the door and stop only when she closes it to leave.

My mother does tests for every conceivable ailment. When my father accused her of being a hypochondriac she scoffed at him, but then rang a hospital to check if she could do a test for it. She takes drugs for everything; drugs she finds in my father's doctor's case, next to his black book of nurse's phone numbers. Yet, she doesn't know what to take for this guilt that she feels. All she can do is speak to her one-eyed astrologer.

You will not believe this, but when my mother suspected I had been raped, she sent me to this same partially sighted astrologer. To this day, she has not told me why. To check if it was an auspicious time to be raped? To check whether my stars were aligned with those of my rapist? If so, could I keep you? Perhaps it was to see if shaving my legs meant I had changed my own destiny. That I brought it on my damn self.

I wanted an abortion, but then you would never have been born, and maybe that would be worse.

'No daughter of mine will terminate a pregnancy,' my father said. 'It disgusts me morally.'

'But you abort babies on a weekly basis for other mothers.'

'Those are for money. Their morals they have to battle with, not mine.'

You were a small baby but I'm told your head was big. The birth was not easy. Later, I will require surgery to stitch some muscles together in my backside. Until then, I break wind without control, and my mother tells me off for 'sending farts', even if we are alone in my hostel room.

'Because I am farting in the daytime, Thathi will not come visit?' I ask my mother. I am only half joking.

They assume my flatulence is another form of rebellion, just like me bringing shame on the family by being raped. It is consigned to the after-hours, at least in name, like all other family secrets; abortions, flirting with nurses, drinking.

'Are you still sending night breezes?' my father asks me whenever we call him from the pay phone.

I have a recurring dream in which I meet you at an airport and it is pitch black outside with a spotlight on us. It is the first time I have seen you since you were taken from me. You are a grown man. A handsome man. You take my hands and kiss my cheeks, and in return, I send you a night breeze.

I know you will find me, and when you do I will look strong. I owe you that. I will not tell you that your father was my rapist, but you're a bright boy. You will find out and you will not know whether to love this man as your father or to hate him for what he did to me.

Because above all else, you love me. I could see that in your eyes. You love me.

My mother says you are in England. 8,778 kilometres away. I know England because my father was sent there twice to upgrade his skills. The first time, they left me with my uncle for two years because they thought I was too small to miss their affection. They were right, but size and age have nothing to do with it. There was no affection to miss. The second time, when I was twelve, for reasons I now appreciate, they took me because they did not want to unfairly tempt my uncle since I had come of age. Even now, I remember the fields of wild strawberries in England; I remember fallen fruits on the grass that I could eat for free. I remember the school lunches – three-course meals everyone else hated but I loved because they offered two more courses than my mother's lunches did. I remember smoking to be fashionable. I remember the lake freezing over and the other school children going sliding across it. I thought that to be so dangerous and never tried it, but now I have dreams of being trapped under the ice, you on the other side of it.

The weather is awful but it's a nice place. You will use your fingers to eat salt-and-vinegar crisps instead of curry. You will have white parents who won't know how to feed you spice; who won't know that they should shave your head to improve your hair growth; they won't know that colic can be overcome with a Buddhist monk's chants; they won't know that dabbing cologne on your head cures all ailments.

But they will feed you meat and make you strong. Strong enough to come back to find me.

I hope you recognize me from across a crowded airport because my mannerisms are yours and we have the same smell. Because, like you, I never sweat. Like you, I want love. I want the warmth my parents cannot provide me.

All I have is hope and a photo of you that the fourteen-year-old maid spent a week's wage to get developed for me.

You are 8,778 kilometres away. It feels like more. But it also feels like less, because I can smell you. My nipples pinch when I think of you. I hear you cry. I love you.

Pot Holiness

A CAMERA FILMS THIS.

It pans around the inside of a marquee that is closed from all sides. The white canvas walls flap with the wind, and there is a determined marching sound of rain on the roof.

The camera zooms in on Conrad Cecil. He is an ugly man, and this is not subjective. He is slightly hunched and has a bulbous nose below his thick glasses and thinning blond hair. This, combined with his great height and expensive teeth, makes him look a great deal more intimidating than the others in his company. He's sitting at a table with two grown Sri Lankan men, Mark and Paul, and one fourteen-year-old blond boy, Mathew. Mathew sparks up a joint and passes it around. The other men smoke without looking up from the piles of money in front of them.

The camera zooms out and then back in on a short, dark man with enormous muscles He is tied to a chair in the corner of the room. His nose is bloody, his eyes swelled shut, his mouth gagged.

Zooming back out, the camera now zeroes in on Conrad Cecil's face, as he rubs tears out of his eyes and says, 'This one hurts the most.' He points towards the man in the chair. 'Chin-up Channa's one of Sri Lanka's forgotten class. A tsunami orphan. Five years ago he was abused by a group of men and nothing was done until those bastards made the mistake of doing the same to a rich man's son. I was called in to do a number on these men and that's when I found Chin-up Channa. We saved you, didn't we, Channa?'

The camera switches to Channa. He nods.

'But because of what those men did to him ...' Camera rotates back to face Conrad Cecil, as fast as possible, overshooting him in the process. He waits till it settles on him to continue. 'Because of what they did to him, he was mute for one hell of a long time. The dude still can't talk in front of women. That kind of pain makes you want to end your own life. Hell, Channa, how many times did you try to off yourself?'

The camera is back on Channa, who holds up three fingers.

'But we found him and we looked after him. 'Changed his life till he became one of Colombo's most sought-after personal trainers,' Conrad Cecil speaks into the lens, 'even though he barely says a bloody word. All because we gave him hope. And what did we ask for in return? Just loyalty. And just loyalty is all this bag of muscles gave us for seven damn years, until now. And you see, ladies and gentlemen, boys and girls, why this is the hardest one for me? I treated him like a son and look what he's trying to do to me to save his own skin. Without me he wouldn't even have any bloody skin. And now he's talked to the cops and because he has, you two punks have jumped on the bandwagon.' Conrad Cecil points his finger at the camera. 'You think you're safe in police custody, but I will get this video to you and when you watch it, remember this: retract everything you've said, and say the cops coerced you or this is what happens to you.' The camera zooms back on to Channa, who is dribbling blood out the side of his mouth. 'Don't forget, the cops were supposed to protect him too.'

It follows Conrad to a long glass table, across which are lined forty-six different types of whiskey and vodka. 'You stay on my side and this is the life we live. So what's it going to be, punks?' He pours shots for Mark and Paul but not Mathew.

'What about me?' asks Mathew.

'You're too young.'

Mathew lifts up the joint and waves it towards the camera. 'Hello.'

'You've loads of lines to remember.' Conrad Cecil looks at the camera. 'Why the hell are you still filming?'

'One more thing,' the camerawoman says. She swerves the camera back to settle once again on the face of Chin-up Channa. The woman's hand enters the frame as it pulls down the cloth tied across his mouth. 'You look like you need something,' she says.

Channa grabs the silver and black crucifix hanging around his neck and shakes his head.

Inside their house, inches from the railway track, Jinesena puts on his security-guard uniform and kisses his sleeping son's head. He sneaks out of the house with his son's bicycle which he will pawn so that he can pay his mounting debts.

Leg-Breaker Gunesekera is at the pawn shop to take the proceeds off him. 'Is this a bloody joke? You're still twenty-two grand short,' he says.

Jinesena smiles. 'I promise I will have it for you by tomorrow.'

'I'm not buying this anymore, man.' Leg-Breaker puts a hand on Jinesena's shoulder and squeezes hard. 'This crap's been going on for three years now. Look, it's not me, okay? I don't get your money to the big man, he's going to send someone to do you some serious harm.'

Jinesena crosses himself. 'I'll have it for you, of that there is no doubt.'

The church hall is less than one hundred metres up the road from where Jinesena works. Every day, for the last two years, some incredibly happy-looking woman standing outside the church has asked him to come inside to meet God. Finally, he is here for his first service.

The church hall is converted from an old tea factory. The floors are wooden. The acoustics are first-class. There are CCTV cameras in every corner, on every beam and column. All seats are taken. Hundreds stand at the back.

A band plays hymns on electric organs and guitars, as those in the crowd scream out the lyrics. Jinesena is shown to a pew near the altar. Next to him is a middle-aged woman with thinning hair and muscular arms. She turns to Jinesena. 'Peace be with you.'

'Good idea,' Jinesena says. Then like a patient in a doctor's waiting room, he asks her, 'What are you here for?'

'I haven't seen my son since he was a baby. Twenty-eight years ago.'

'You will find him, of that I am sure.'

'No, that's not what I want,' she says. 'He has to find me.'

A bald man, dark and big-bearded, moves amongst the congregation with a microphone and when he lifts his hand, the music stops. The camera follows him as he gets up on stage.

'I am Kalu Baba. All I demand of you is the truth in God's eyes. Only then can you be cured by our prophet, our leader, our salvation. For we have all sinned. Every man, woman and child in this here hall.'

Kalu Baba ambles up to the front row of the congregation where six blind men sit. 'It's obvious what you people need. Peace and God's praise be with you.'

'And also with you.'

'Within an hour of our prophet arriving, you will no longer need those canes. Instead you will have the Lord's vision.' Kalu Baba ambles up to the lady sitting next to Jinesena.

'I am still looking for my son,' she says.

'And the prophet knows that you want him to find you. Can the Prophet guide Sidhara?' Kalu Baba asks the congregation.

'He can and He shall.'

The lady drops money into the collection bag.

Next, the camera is in the face of a man with a twenty-thousand-rupee haircut, the kind you only see in posters for hair products – layered, wavy, spiked. 'My name is Danuja, and I want my family back.'

'How much do you want them back?' Kalu Baba asks.

'More than anything,' Danuja says.

'Can the Prophet bring them back?'

'He can and He shall,' the congregation shouts.

Danuja places a one-hundred-thousand-rupee cash cheque in the collection bag.

Kalu Baba comes back to Jinesena and holds the microphone to his face. 'Tell us who you are and what you need.'

'My name is Jinesena. I am just here to meet you all.'

'In this place of worship, we are all friends,' Kalu Baba says. He looks up to the roof of the hall. 'I can sense you are in debt. Is this correct?'

'Yes,' Jinesena says.

The crowd gasps.

Kalu Baba says, 'I have never met you before, so you could never have told me about your debt. Is that true?'

'Yes,' Jinesena says.

The crowd gasps again.

'But,' Jinesena says, 'I filled out a form in which I mentioned this.' The microphone is too far from his face to pick up what he says.

'You owe money to a debt collector who will kill you if you do not pay up,' says Kalu Baba. 'Then who will look after your son?'

'I don't want to die,' Jinesena says.

'Can the Prophet save this man's life?'

'He can and He shall.'

Jinesena drops two hundred rupees in the collection bag, leaving him with even less money to pay his debts.

Kalu Baba signals to a man on the balcony above the congregation. As the lights go off, everyone is silent.

In surround sound, there is thunder resounding from the speakers. The wooden floor rumbles. 'He is coming, my friends, he is coming.'

Jinesena holds on tight to the chair in front of him.

Spotlights glare on two men on either side of the stage.

The first man says, 'Numbers 12:6; He said, "Hear now My words: If there is a prophet among you, I, the Lord, shall make Myself known to him in a vision. I shall speak with him in a dream."'

The second man says, 'Josiah 12:10; I have also spoken to the Prophets, and I gave them vision, and through the prophets I gave parables.'

'Ladies and gentlemen,' says Kalu Baba. 'Put your hands together for our preachers. Two men who have returned from the dark side with God's light. Two men who can speak our words to the Lord. Two men who are here to welcome you, to guide you, to introduce you to our prophet. Oh behold, my friends, shut out the world. Close your eyes and remain in silence as we wait for the prince of peace, the lord of mercy, our prophet.'

Jinesena follows instructions.

Conrad Cecil takes off his shirt and hangs it from the back of his chair. He is now alone with Mathew and Channa.

'You know your lines, big guy?' Conrad Cecil asks Mathew.

'Better than I know my own face,' says Mathew.

'We have to get this right.'

'Have I ever got it wrong?'

Conrad Cecil smiles, lights a cigarette, takes a drag, then puts it in Channa's mouth so he can take a puff. He squats in front of his captive. 'I want to let you go in peace, my son, but I can't. I'm sorry it had to come to this but I can't let you have your day in court.'

'Sir, please,' Channa says. 'I'll tell them I was lying.'

Conrad Cecil kisses Channa on both cheeks. 'Once you join, you can't leave us.'

'I know, sir, I never would.'

'Then what exactly do you want?' Conrad Cecil asks.

'I want to be forgiven.'

'Me too,' says Conrad Cecil. He puts on a crisp white shirt with a Chinese collar. 'Me too. I shall ask for both of us when I get to church.' He puts his hand around Channa's neck.

Out of the darkness of the church hall, Jinesena follows a spotlight until it shines on a fourteen-year-old blond boy. He is kneeling in front of Kalu Baba and between the two men on either side of the stage. He says, 'Jeremiah 1:14-16, Then the Lord said to me, "Out of the north the evil will break forth on all the inhabitants of the land. For, behold, I am calling all the families of the kingdoms of the north," declares the Lord; "and they will come and they will set each one his throne at the entrance of the gates of Jerusalem, and against all its walls round about and against all the cities of Judah. I will pronounce My judgements on them concerning all their wickedness, whereby they have forsaken Me and have offered sacrifices to other gods, and worshipped the works of their own hands."'

The camera zooms in on the blond boy whose image is projected on giant screens around the hall. He rolls his eyeballs back so all the congregation can see is white and his body shakes as if in a trance. 'There is one God, ladies and gentlemen, and he speaks to me. Has spoken to me since I was four. Has taught me his words, has communicated through me, has helped me cure and heal and teach and punish.' He lifts his hands. 'All with these child's hands. And last night he spoke to me of his prophet. The one true prophet of the one true God, and that prophet is here tonight to bless you, to cure you and to rid you of evil. He is our modern-day saviour, our Jesus, our reason to be. Please welcome, ladies and gentlemen ...' The boy has to stop speaking as the stomping of feet on the wooden floor has become too overpowering. 'Please welcome, the one, the only, our Lord, our oxygen, a gentle subservient master of all that is good, returning from the U S of A for the first time in two months, because God told him of your need. Please my friends, my family, my people, recognize the only one amongst us who has never sinned. All raise your hands and say Hallelujah for our prophet.'

The congregation stands and shouts, 'Hallelujah.'

'Hallelujah,' Jinesena shouts, but everyone else is already sitting down again.

A tall white man struts his way onto the stage, clasping his hands together in front of him. He lifts his arms above his head and everyone in the crowd roars their approval. While he takes centre stage, Jinesena notices a spot of blood on the man's Chinese collar.

The white man notices him looking and points to it himself. He beckons for the camera to focus on it so that everyone can see on the big screens. 'Blood, but it is not mine,' the white man says. 'Blood, but I have not cut myself. Blood, the tears of your pain, the sign of your suffering. I am here to bleach that blood away.' He puts his hand around a concealed earpiece. 'I am here to cure blindness, pay debts, and reunite families. I am your prophet and my name is Conrad Cecil.'

White Knight

GAYAN SCAMPERED INTO the froth of a dying wave, blinking at the setting sun's reflection on the turquoise sea. Fishermen in catamarans fought to bring their catch under control as clouds encroached on the red-tinged Negombo sky. The monsoon breeze, whistling through the gaps in the palm leaves, dropped a vendor's frangipani at Gayan's feet as he watched a sunburnt woman clamber up an elephant's raised leg. The mahout, tucking a bundle of cash into his sarong, flashed the tourist a toothless smile and poked at the elephant with what looked like a devil's trident.

With his gaze shifting between the elephant and the turds it had just released like cluster bombs, Gayan stepped on a burrow in the sand, which crumbled under his weight. A crab scurried out, went up the beach towards the point where the girl of Gayan's dreams stood wringing water from her blond hair. She wore a blue bikini top which looked like small sails stretched across giant masts. As she lifted her green-and-orange beach wrap, it fanned out in the wind like a peacock's tail.

Gayan stood next to her, a frangipani extended in front of him, but everything he had planned to say was lost like the crab without its home.

She snapped her fingers in his face and said, 'You're a feisty little chappy. If this keeps happening, one day I'll –'

'One day you'll what?' Gayan grinned, his palms raised in prayer.

'One day I may have to find your parents and tell them that you're chasing twenty-two-year-old ladies.'

'But you're the most beautiful woman I've ever seen,' he said, 'and I've seen lots of women in my time.'

'You're just a kid.'

'The age of consent in Sri Lanka is twelve,' Gayan said.

'So you keep telling me, but I looked it up. A couple of years ago, they changed it to sixteen.'

One of Gayan's palms deflected the slap from the other. 'Just my luck.'

The blonde grinned. 'Doesn't mean anything would have happened if the laws had stayed the same.'

'Why'd you look it up then?'

'Good question,' she said. 'Because I didn't think it was possible that anyone could be sick enough to assume twelve-year-olds could consent.'

'I'm fourteen.' Gayan puffed out his chest. 'I know what I'm doing.'

'I'm sure you think you do. Is that frangipani for me?' She sniffed it from his hand. 'Wow. That's heaven on a stem.'

'I can get you more.'

'One day, love,' she said. 'One day, you'll be a hunk of a man, but by then I'll be old and wrinkly.'

'You're not that old.'

'Compared to you I am.' She kissed Gayan on the cheek.

'I'll never wash my face.' He cupped his mouth with his hands. 'Can you do me a tiny favour?'

'Depends.'

'If any of my friends ask, can you say we're meeting tonight?'

She shook her head. 'I could get arrested for something like that.'

'Not if nobody knows about it.'

'But you just told me to tell your friends.'

'Okay, we won't tell anyone,' he said.

'Never going to happen.'

'I understand. The laws.' Gayan covered his face with his hands, before opening them like the doors of a cuckoo clock. 'Sea Spray Guest House, second floor, third room on the right. No pressure.' His heels dug into the sand as he turned and sprinted off.

Gayan re-joined his teammates for a game of beach cricket.

An Englishman, standing behind a mounted video camera, loosened his old-school bow tie. He dived after his straw hat when the wind knocked it off his head, but it escaped him and swooped towards the sea before the wicket-keeper trapped it under his foot.

The man tucked his shirt back into his Bermuda shorts and flicked sand off his knee-high striped socks. 'Thank you so much, young man,' he said when the wicket-keeper returned his hat to him. 'What's your name?'

The wicket-keeper smiled, crossed his arms and said, 'Good morning. I love you. Happy birthday.'

Gayan cracked up as all the boys gathered around him, slapping each other on the back, giggling with little or no control.

The man stood with his palms out. 'Sorry, I don't think I got the joke.'

'Sir,' Gayan said, before taking a few deep breaths. 'He just repeated the only words he knows in English because he had no idea what you asked him.'

The man's broad shoulders flexed up and down as he laughed. 'That is rather funny.' He reached his hand out and said, 'Steven Mathews.'

'Oh my god. The Steven Mathews?'

Mathews nodded.

'I'm Gayan Galapitage.'

Mathews closed his eyes and clicked his fingers. 'I know that name. You've just been picked for Sri Lanka under-fifteens?'

'Correct, sir.' Gayan leaned his head to one side and smiled. 'Plus, I open the batting for Western Province Juniors.'

'I'm guessing you're here for the all-island schools' cricket final. Staying the night, are you?'

'Yes, sir,' Gayan said. 'Two in fact.'

'I saw Imran Khan play for Oxford when he must have been about five years older than you are now. You look very much like he did then. Same strong jaw.'

'Thank you, sir.'

'Well, I'll be at your match tomorrow.' Mathews pointed towards a fat man lying face down in the sand. 'Your coach is helping me select three boys to take to England to play club cricket.'

'That's the first I've heard of it, sir.'

Mathews laughed and ruffled Gayan's hair. 'I'm not very good at keeping secrets.'

To no one's great surprise, Gayan rose to the occasion and was man of the final. Despite this, Coach Silva had not mentioned anything to him about Steven Mathews and the opportunity to play in England. Against his better instincts, Gayan felt the need to challenge him about this. So while his friends took to the beach, Gayan went looking for him. He crossed the road amidst a cacophony of musical car horns, whilst a lop-sided public bus sprayed him with powdery exhaust fumes. Street vendors covered their ware in plastic sheets and motorcyclists gathered under the patched-up roof of an unmanned military checkpoint.

Standing at the guest house's gate, Gayan looked down at the one inch of muddy water in the swimming pool they had been promised would be in use. Since it wasn't, he tried to use the shower to wash off the stickiness of the salt water and sea air, but it spluttered out rusty sludge. A cloud of mosquitoes hovered above his head, convincing him to take the longer path to the main building so that he wouldn't become yet another statistic in the dengue epidemic.

The thunder came, sounding like the bombs they claimed were confined to the north. The breeze cooled as spitting rain drops dampened Gayan's shirt.

He tapped on the glass-door entrance to Coach Uncle's room.

'Enter.'

Gayan tiptoed towards the trophy they had won that morning. The only bulb in the room hung above the ceiling fan; the room flickered between light and dark on the whim of the fan's blades.

'Hello,' Gayan said as he clapped his hands together to kill a mosquito. 'Sir?'

'Channa?'

'No, it's me, Gayan. Can I talk to you?'

Coach Uncle rose from his bed, behind a cloud of smoke and a mosquito net. He sipped at a milky liquid in a plastic bottle. 'Want some toddy?' he asked, squeezing the bottle through a hole in the net.

'No, thank you, sir.'

'Don't know how things work with you rich people, but where I come from, if offered something by an elder, rude not to take.'

Gayan grabbed the bottle with both hands, closed his eyes and took a swig of the drink, spitting out an insect in the process.

'Forgot to tell you to watch out for flies and ants,' Coach Uncle said. 'Natural drink, sapped from palm trees. Filter the insects through your teeth.'

Gayan took another sip of the thick, white liquid. 'Is this alcoholic?'

'Do popes shit in the woods?' Coach Uncle said. 'Or do I mean bears?'

'I feel funny, sir.'

'You'll get over it.' Coach Uncle looked him up and down. 'Why you here?'

'Sir, I know about Steven Mathews.'

'Say what?'

'About the club cricket in the UK. About the boys you told him to take.'

'Yes, all good players.'

'One of them was Channa, no? That guy we played against today.'

'The leg-spinner, yes.'

'I destroyed him. Smashed him round the park.'

'He had a poor day, sure.'

'But you didn't give my name to Mathews.'

Coach Uncle patted down the four hairs on his head and walked towards Gayan, his double-chin inching into the natural light offered through the glass door. He wore a spider-web-print sarong and a stained-white vest that looked like a bra above his rice belly. His eyelids kept flickering, offering brief glimpses of the chilli red of his eyes.

Gayan dropped to his knees and air-kissed Coach Uncle's feet.

Coach Uncle passed him more toddy. 'Big boy now. Batted like a beauty today. Deserve to celebrate. One day it will be champagne. Today toddy.'

'But, sir –'

'Don't ruin things. Best day of my life, Gayan,' Coach Uncle said. 'Six years in charge of Colombo College's under-fourteens, first bloody trophy. Drink up, boy.' Coach Uncle lit a beedi. 'Want some?'

Gayan reluctantly took a drag and held the smoke in his mouth for a few moments, before he released it all in one cough.

'Look around you, boy,' Coach Uncle said. 'What do you see?'

'I don't know, sir. It's dark.'

Coach Uncle shook his head and asked, 'Then what do you smell?'

'Smell, sir? Not sure. Um, the sea?'

'What else, boy?'

'The fish? My sweat? Exhaust fumes. My ...' Gayan closed his eyes, feeling like he did when he sat for school exams for which he hadn't studied.

'Smell your hands, boy,' Coach Uncle said.

'Leather smell.'

'The smell of money?' Coach Uncle asked.

'No, sir,' Gayan said.

'The smell in the air?'

Gayan breathed in deeply through his nose. 'I don't know.'

'Burning,' Coach Uncle said. 'I can smell uprising. You rich bastards try to trample on my people.'

'Sir, but –'

'I have a problem, boy. Lost my trust in you when you played that idiot shot this morning. Doesn't matter how many runs you scored.'

'We won, sir,' Gayan said, the room spinning around him.

'Trained you hard. Taught you to be a man, but you played that bastard baby shot. Trying to impress some sweet bitch in the crowd?'

Gayan wiped sweat off his forehead and looked down at Coach Uncle's feet.

'Winning isn't the only thing. Hitting Channa around the park is not the only goddamn thing. Other teams say I have a rich boy I can't control.' Coach Uncle picked up the trophy, lifting it over his head. 'Winner of the championship mocked because he can't handle his bloody spoilt brat. You have to respect me. Have to respect the game. Why aren't you drinking?'

Gayan took another sip of toddy.

'Can't endorse you to Mathews unless I can trust you. But how?' Coach Uncle asked. 'Can leave it like this. Or can punish you and then maybe I'll forget this and trust you again. What do you want, son?'

'Sir, please judge me by the runs I score.'

'Channa never answers back, you know. Sure he makes mistakes. Sure he bowls like crap sometimes, but he doesn't complain and he makes no excuses. Bugger lost his whole family in the tsunami. Lives in a goddamn orphanage but he never complains. Never gets jealous. And when I have to punish him, he takes it like a man and just gets on with life.'

'Punish me, sir,' Gayan said. 'If that helps you forget.'

Coach Uncle kicked away dirty clothes on the floor and found a wicker cane which he slapped against his own palm. As he pulled the curtain across the open glass door, dust blew out against him. 'Bend down, son.'

'Sir, I thought –'

'Do you want to play in England or not?'

'Okay, sir.' He bent forward. The only light in the room snuck in through a rip in the curtain. He heard the whistle of the first slash of the cane but the pain took time to develop. It felt like it did when a jellyfish had stung him when he was nine: a sharp, burning sensation. Gayan wrapped his lips around his teeth to keep himself from being too loud. *Be strong,* he told himself. *Be strong. International cricketers don't cry after a beating.*

The cane dropped to the floor. 'Turn this way, son.' Coach Uncle put his arms around Gayan, and kissed the top of his head. 'Sorry. Best way for you to learn.'

Gayan rubbed his tears against Coach Uncle's vest, realizing this to be a mistake almost immediately. Coach Uncle's body odour was stale smoke and toddy sweat, urine and vomit.

'Hope that hurt and left a scar. In eight years or so, maybe you'll lift the World Cup. Can look at these scars and they'll tell you of the struggles it took to get there. Understand?'

'I do,' Gayan said, not believing it for one second.

Coach Uncle locked the glass door and picked up a torch. 'Let's look at your scars then.'

'Sir, they're under my shorts.'

Coach Uncle sniggered, lifted his shoulders and covered his face with his hands. 'You play international cricket, you'll have much harder things to do than show scars to your beloved coach. Only asking you to show me where it hurts. Scared?'

'I'm never scared, sir.' Gayan tried to hide the trembling of his hands as he pulled down his shorts to expose his scars.

'Knew it would be hard to see red bruises in this light.' Coach Uncle bent down low enough for Gayan to be able to feel warm breath on his backside. 'Maybe I better come closer.'

'No, sir.' Gayan pulled up his shorts and turned around to face Coach Uncle. 'Please don't. I beg of you, sir, please don't.'

'Son, playing for the national side, boys will rag you. Must be prepared.'

'Please.' Gayan backed away towards the bathroom. 'I'll try much harder next time.'

Coach Uncle laughed again. 'You're acting like you're scared of me.'

'I'm not acting, sir. I'm begging.' Tears flooded down Gayan's face. The room appeared to dance around him like the growing flames of a bushfire.

'Come on, baba. This is important for your development. Soon you'll be playing with adults.'

'I'll quit cricket, sir.'

Coach Uncle shook his head and said, 'Have another sip, and behave like a man.'

Gayan took two unsteady steps towards the bottle and fell into Coach Uncle's arms.

'Never disobey your coach. That's rule number one, you ungrateful bastard bitch. Gave you a chance and this is how you repay me?'

Coach Uncle grabbed at the back of Gayan's hair and powered his head into a rattan shelf. Something snapped.

Gayan opened his eyes; his head pounded and his tongue felt like sandpaper against the inside of his cheeks. Slime green and mustard yellow bathroom tiles surrounded him. The toilet was a squatting pan, crusty faeces and thick urine around it. He needed to use it, but he had no control over his limbs. Warm liquid trickled down his leg, but he couldn't scream because he was trying to be a man about this. A cockroach scurried over his feet and a squadron of red ants marched over the ridges of his abdominal muscles, which is when he noticed he was semi-naked.

He looked out through a cracked window. On the beach across the road, a batsman top-edged a pull shot, lofting the ball miles in the air. The wicket-keeper ran after it, his hair flapping in the wind, taking the catch over his shoulder, diving forward into the sea. His teammates squealed around him like the mosquitoes that sucked at Gayan's ankles.

Steven Mathews filmed the game and clapped his approval.

Gayan had to close his eyes again.

Coach Uncle coughed. 'Kept me waiting a long time, boy.' He dragged Gayan into the bedroom. 'No fighting now.'

Gayan breathed in deeply through his nose and tried to make a dash for the door. Without skipping a beat, Coach Uncle threw him against a wall and dug his elbow into his spine.

'Heads, you try that again and I snip-snip your dick. Tails, behave and play in England. What's it going to be, bad boy?'

Coach Uncle lifted his sarong, and tied it up again; he splashed talcum powder under his armpits and spat into his own hands.

Gayan turned away to face the glass door and could see through the rip in the curtain. Outside, Steven Mathews undid his bow tie as he went about knocking on doors around the pool.

'Help,' Gayan shouted, but with too much hesitance and too little breath to be heard.

Coach Uncle put a hand to Gayan's mouth and looked over his shoulder and out the window. 'Keep your bloody bastard mouth shut or I'll take out your silver spoon and shove it up your ass.'

Coach Uncle grabbed a tennis ball from his kit bag on the floor and squeezed it between his hairy fingers, before wedging it into Gayan's mouth.

Gayan could feel the corners of his lips stretching open, as sticky saliva dripped out of his mouth. He tried to scream but his mouth was jammed wide open, so his whimper had no carry.

But Coach Uncle heard and he responded by punching the tennis ball deeper into Gayan's mouth, making him gag. 'Don't try that shit again, boy.'

Gayan looked through the curtain once more and saw Mathews coming closer. He knew he had to get the attention of his white knight. He pretended to trip back against the glass of the window; it didn't shatter, but it made a hollow noise like one beat of a drum.

Mathews turned towards the noise, took off his straw hat and wiped raindrops off his thick glasses. He leaned on his walking stick and hobbled towards Coach Uncle's room. 'Hello,' he said, banging on the locked door. 'Hello.'

'Keep quiet, boy,' Coach Uncle said, switching off his torch and tucking his vest back into his sarong. 'Make any noise and I'll slice off your lips.'

Mathews fiddled with the handle on the main door, but gave up after a few seconds and turned to walk away.

Gayan knew he had one final chance. His elbow was centimetres from an empty bottle of arrack on a table by the window. He looked through the curtains again and saw Mathews shielding his pipe from the rain.

It was a matter of seconds before he would be gone. Gayan dived at the table, tackling its legs so that the bottle slid off and smashed against the floor next to his head. Shards of glass bounced against his cheeks, before coming to rest on the floor.

Coach Uncle lifted Gayan back to his feet. 'Stay still, little bastard.'

Mathews waddled back towards the room. He fiddled with the handle on the glass door and something clicked. A splinter of light bisected the room as the curtains blew in with the wind. Mathews looked towards Gayan, removed his glasses, rubbed his eyes and then looked again.

'Who did this?' he asked as he tried to pull the tennis ball out of Gayan's mouth. Gayan muffled some noises and pointed with his eyes towards Coach Uncle, who rose to his feet out of Mathews' shadow.

Gayan spat out the last of the tennis ball and in the same breath said, 'Behind you, behind you, behind you, beh –'

Mathews turned and raised his walking stick in defence. 'Coach, what the hell?'

'I can explain.' A clap of thunder interrupted a smiling Coach Uncle.

'You stupid idiot,' Mathews said. 'What have you gone and done? What have you gone and done. You've ruined everything.'

Gayan gasped for air and spat out yellow tennis ball threads.

'Not what you think it is,' Coach Uncle said. 'Didn't touch the boy. Just punished him for that stupid shot. Just explained why I didn't endorse him.'

'But where's –'

'Channa hasn't come yet, sir.'

'And you replaced him with Gayan?'

'Never did anything to Gayan.'

'Look at him, man, look at him.' Mathews banged his walking stick against the ground. 'You have no idea who this boy's father is, do you? You bloody idiot.'

Smiling, Mathews shuffled towards Gayan, stared into his eyes and stroked his hair. 'What a beautiful young boy. It was never meant to be you.' He yanked at Gayan's hair and rammed the tennis ball back into his mouth.

Lovable Idiot

WHEN JINESENA PUTS on his Monsoon Lodge security guard uniform for the first time, his seven-year-old son salutes him and asks, 'How many bad guys are you going to catch today?'

Jinesena holds up nine fingers.

'No way, Thathi, that's too cool.'

Jinesena has never told his son that he is a policeman but he has never told him that he isn't either. He certainly looks the part dressed in khaki trousers tucked into knee-length boots, a white shirt with a black tie and a grey jacket with mock medals sewn onto it.

Nalaka can speak English, but he can't read it. If he could, he would have seen that his father's badge says Monsoon Lodge Trainee Security Officer on it. Still, Jinesena is proud of himself because he is going to be bringing home a salary and not just living off his wife's remittance from her job as a maid in Saudi Arabia. At the end of the month he is meant to receive a pay cheque for seventeen thousand rupees. This is about half of what his wife earns, but he does not have to go through the torment she does at the hands of her employers. Before he became a guard, Jinesena had justified his lack of work by saying that bringing up Nalaka was a full-time job. His wife had no idea he was not working until she came back for her first visit in three years. She was angry enough at this deception to say that she would not send him any more money until he showed her proof of employment. When she returned to the Middle East, Nalaka lost his mother again, and even though she left him a skateboard as a gift, he envied those of his friends whose mothers were maids to rich creeps in Colombo.

As it turned out, Jinesena sold his son's skateboard to pay back the man who had got him the job at Monsoon Lodge. Nalaka spent two days believing his father's assertion that the army had taken his skateboard for one of their missions, but when he learnt the truth he howled for hours. He didn't know how to ride the thing, but because his mother had given it to him it was his prized possession. He even slept with it, allocating space on the few inches of torn foam that he used as a mattress.

'Putha, I had to pay that money or my job would be lost.'

Nalaka dragged his nails down his father's legs. 'Ammi will hammer you when she finds out.'

'She won't find out because she's not here. She has left everything for me to do.'

'Well, if you made any money she wouldn't have to go away.'

Jinesena raised a hand to threaten his boy against such insolence, yet he knew that he had failed his wife and son. He fell to the floor and pulled at his own hair. 'I'm sorry, putha, I'm sorry.'

Nalaka crawled towards him and rested a palm on his father's shoulder. 'What's wrong, Thathi?'

'You have no pride in me.'

'No,' Nalaka said, patting his father on the back. 'But I love you.'

Now, things are different. Standing tall in his new uniform, Jinesena asks his son, 'Would you like a new skateboard or a shiny bike?'

Nalaka flashes stained teeth. 'A shiny bike. A shiny bike.'

'Soon, boy, soon. Let me wait till the bike I have in mind for you becomes available.'

Nalaka tugs at his father's arms. 'What bike, Thathi? What bike is it?'

Jinesena thinks to himself, *a bike someone will give me for free*, but he says, 'A big black bike.'

'With a basket for my school books?'

'Nothing less.'

'Lights like Susil Uncle's?'

Jinesena beams a smile, enjoying this as much as his son. He lifts the boy above his head. 'Lights bigger than his. Flashing lights too.'

'Is it a police bike from your work?'

'It is just like one, putha, but I am making it especially so that it can be your size. That is why I need time.'

After work Jinesena, a man of his word, as long as his word is affordable, visits the bike shop opposite his work. He makes sure the security guard who opens the door for him can see his hat. Running the gates for Monsoon Lodge is infinitely more impressive than opening the door at a bike shop. The two guards have a stand-off, but then they smile, respecting each other for their commitment to the safety of others.

Jinesena asks for the owner, Mr Krishan, who turns out to be a portly man with buck teeth. He points him towards the kids' bike area where Jinesena's primary goal is to check prices. Each bike is at least four times his budget, yet he says, 'How reasonable. Do you accept credit cards?'

'Yes,' Mr Krishan says, his head turned to the side. 'You have one?'

'Many,' Jinesena says, yet the closest thing he has to a credit card is the cardboard cut-out of an American Express card that came with the fake-leather wallet he bought in Pettah.

He leaves empty-handed, but returns every other day for a week until he plucks up the courage to tell Mr Krishan that times are hard and to ask if he has any bikes for one thousand rupees. Mr Krishan laughs for a little then kicks him out and asks him never to return again.

Every day, Nalaka comes running down the road to see if his father has the bike. Each disappointment is accompanied by a tsunami of tears, so much so that Jinesena wonders how his son has any tears left.

Jinesena and Nalaka live in a shack made of corrugated iron, inches from a road that more and more people use to avoid traffic in the city. A railway track runs behind them, but the noise of trains feels comforting, rather than disturbing.

If Nalaka's tears aren't running dry, Jinesena's excuses certainly are. Of course he wants his son to believe his lies, but he begins to worry that he is far too gullible. Is there something wrong with Nalaka? Is he a lovable idiot like Susil Uncle? Even though Nalaka is just seven, how many times can he believe that the bike is needed by the shortest officer for an emergency police operation? Jinesena knows he can come up with better excuses but he doesn't seem to need to.

Sure he feels guilty, never more so than when he tells him he left the bike outside their house and someone stole it. Nalaka runs between the sheet-metal shacks within the shanty, shouting for the bike to be returned, promising that if it isn't his father will caution everyone. It is a good thing, Jinesena thinks, that Nalaka doesn't notice people saying things like, 'Oh, how scary, the gate opener will chase us.'

His son's credulousness almost makes Jinesena complacent. He forgets the bike altogether until he passes Mr Krishan on the way to work.

'I have a child's bike I can let go for two thousand,' Mr Krishan says. 'That is as cheap as I will ever go.'

Jinesena doesn't bother to bargain as he knows this to be a good price. But he doesn't have the money and even though salaries are due in a couple of days, he has taken so many advances that he will only receive an empty envelope.

'Can I have the bike on credit?' he asks.

Mr Krishan smiles and says, 'Let me think about it.' He rubs his chin. 'I have thought about it and no you can't.'

'Please can you hold on to it till I get the money?'

'You have four days after which the price will go up or I will sell to someone else.'

That evening when Jinesena returns again with no bike, Nalaka drops to his knees with his hands up in prayer. 'Do you really have a bike for me, Thathi?' He flicks his greasy curls out of his eyes. 'My friend's father says you have no money and you're lying.'

'Which friend?'

'Kusal. Uncle Dilshan's son.'

Jinesena clenches his fists. Dilshan is a real police officer. 'I have a bike, putha, I swear on my life. But it's not right for you yet. I have my people at the station working on it.'

'Uncle Dilshan says you don't work at the station.'

Jinesena grabs Nalaka by his mud-soaked collar. 'Dilshan is too junior to even know what I do.' Jinesena looks around. 'I cannot tell you anymore as it may put you in danger.'

'Danger from whom, Thathi?'

'Would you believe me if I said dinosaurs?'

Jinesena has three days to raise the money. He doesn't much care for lying but he has got used to it, and each time he tells an untruth he feels less guilty. So now he has a new scam. When he opens the car doors for members of the Monsoon Lodge, he starts to charm them. 'You look nice today, sir.' 'Madam, have you lost even more weight?' And to the whitest members: 'You tan so well!'

This is the set-up, but it is taking him nowhere and he only has one day left to buy the bike, so the lies need to be more dramatic. 'My daughter was in an accident, but I cannot afford to pay the hospital fees.'

Jinesena does not have a daughter, but he thought if he said his son was in an accident he would be tempting fate. Yet, as dishonest as he is being, the odd hundred here and there is never going to break the bank of some linen-clad, gin-and-tonic sipping expat on a cushy tropical gig. Jinesena maintains his morals in other ways. For example, when a rich guy, driving an MG, offers him five hundred bucks to spy on a member, for reasons he is not privy to, Jinesena says no.

Instead, Jinesena maintains his ethics and raises the money he needs by lying about his fictitious daughter. He gets home late that night, and Nalaka is already asleep but he wakes him up.

'Putha, putha.'

Nalaka rubs his eyes. 'Is it morning?'

'No, little man, but guess what I will bring home for you tomorrow?'

Nalaka bolts upright. 'My bike?'

'Yes, your bike.' Jinesena flashes the money at his son. 'It is all ready and this is the money to pay for it.'

'I knew you weren't lying, Thathi.' Nalaka throws his arms around his father. 'Are you the best father in the world?'

'Some say that it is so.' Jinesena feels like a million rupees. He may not be a cop, but his son thinks he is and loves him for it.

Yet, when he gets to the bike shop the next day, Mr Krishan smiles and says, 'You're a day late. Price goes up.'

'But I have exactly what you asked for.'

'Which you got pretty easily.'

'I refuse to pay a cent over two thousand two hundred.'

Mr Krishan turns his back. 'Well good luck explaining to your son why you have come home again with no bike.'

Mr Krishan does the buttons up on his shirt and exits the shop. 'I'm going for some food. Come back tomorrow with two thousand eight hundred and I will give you the bike, the basket and the lights.'

The bike shop guard opens the door for Mr Krishan and follows him out, so that he can direct his car into traffic. Mr Krishan's assistant whistles away in the storeroom so Jinesena feels pretty confident he is alone up front. As if in some sort of trance, he feels the room emptying. Everything vanishes, except for the black bike for Nalaka. Basket attached. Lights attached. Next door, the church bells chime and organ music filters into the shop with a beam of sunlight. Jinesena imagines God whispering, 'Take the bike. It's yours.'

Yet, Jinesena is no thief. He could have given his son so many more things if he was, but what kind of lesson would that be? Jinesena is a security guard and he cannot let down other guards who stand for the same code of honour as he does. So he rolls the bike to the front of the shop, and opens the glass door. The bell rings.

Mr Krishan's assistant calls out from the storeroom, 'One minute.'

Jinesena lifts the bike onto the road. The other guard sees him and comes running back, abandoning his boss. 'What the hell are you doing, brother?'

Jinesena stands up straight, clicks his shoes and salutes. 'Please accept my apologies.' He throws two thousand two hundred rupees at him, mounts the bicycle and pedals off furiously.

Jinesena realizes he looks ridiculous in full uniform on a child's bike which is hardly moving below his rice belly, even though his legs are going at a hundred miles an hour. Eventually he gathers momentum down a sloping street which leads to the rail track and the sea.

At the bottom of the street, Jinesena hops off the bike and carries it into a deserted building site for an aborted hotel project. With as many as forty floors on which to hide the bike, he can do the needful, then climb over the wall and go back to work at Monsoon Lodge. After his shift, he will return and collect the bike for his lovable son.

Once he finds the perfect hiding spot, Jinesena comes out of the building, but he doubles back when he sees Mr Krishan marching down the road. All Jinesena has to do is jump back into the building and hide, but just as he is about to do so a white teenager, blond hair dripping with sea water and blood, calls out, 'Please, man, you gotta help. Please, guard.'

Jinesena knows that, as a security guard, he is a hero. A saviour. The white boy needs saving.

'What is it, son?' Jinesena asks.

'My friend's drowning. Please, please come quick.'

Jinesena takes a deep breath, and imagines what he would do if it was Nalaka drowning. He has to save the white boy's friend so he leaps out of the building, over the train tracks and onto the rocks set out to hold the waves at bay. The white boy points out a few yards. His friend, likely Sri Lankan and about twenty years old, is holding on with the tips of his fingers to a rock a few metres out. The waves are pummelling into him.

'I tried to save him,' the white boy says, 'but the current's too strong. It dragged me down.'

Jinesena unclips his tie, throws off his hat, jacket and shirt and kicks off his shoes. 'Stand aside.'

He clambers down two relatively dry rocks, but the next one is covered in green slime. He slips into the water, cracking the small of his back against something hard. The current drags him under and turns him round and round. He has salt up his nose, through his brain, out his ears.

He closes his eyes.

At that moment, he knows it is hopeless. This is the end; Nalaka will never see his bike and he will remember his father to be the loser that he is. Jinesena can't let that happen. He will never ever give up, so he opens his eyes and thrashes around with his arms until his head is above water again. He takes in a breath, sees the white boy's brown friend still on the rock, and then the current sucks him under again and he is ready to give up after all. This time he is sure he is dead. Trapped below the surface. Never to see his wife again, but he doesn't like her much anyway. Never to see his darling boy again, which is much harder to accept.

Everything is silent. The end of a song. The end of life. Calm.

And just like that, everything is noisy, chaotic. People screaming, people clapping, Jinesena's body being dragged out of the water. His head hanging limp off his bruised shoulders. Below him, the smile of a man with the biggest arms he has ever seen. The face of the man who saved his life. The face of Cuckoo Siva, one of the most powerful men in Sri Lanka, rumoured to be romantically involved with Madam President. And here he is dragging a lowly security guard like Jinesena out of the water.

Then he is gone.

Jinesena doesn't have time to work out if this is just a dream. Before he knows it, two cops, real ones, are bundling him into a police car with his hands cuffed. Outside, Mr Krishan hurls abuse at him and demands to know where the bike is. Jinesena is in la la land, so just smiles and waves. A few moments later, wearing his soaking wet trousers, but dry tie, jacket and hat, he slumps in the corner of a room at Kollupitiya police station. It is the instinct which comes with the uniform which makes him sure that the men around him, in handcuffs, must have broken the law. Despite his situation, all he can think about is how he will tell his son about meeting Cuckoo Siva.

Six hours later, the officer-in-charge of the 'Cop Shed' leads Jinesena into his room and offers him tea and a cigarette. Outside, a booming voice asks, 'Where is the idiot?'

Cuckoo Siva stands at the door. The first thing Jinesena notices is how amazing he smells. Aftershave so expensive it must have its own mortgage – so floral, yet so manly, and so strong it overpowers the musty smell in the office. He is wearing a white linen shirt and blue jeans, both so well pressed you would need a forensic team to find a single crease. He has a thick gold chain around his neck, with a diamond-encrusted dumbbell pendant. He pulls out a comb, brushing back his hair, which if Jinesena is honest, looks like a wig or a hair transplant because it hangs too low on his forehead.

Jinesena drops to his knees, head bowed, shuffling towards his hero like a dog who has been caught with his master's favourite slipper in his mouth. He kisses Cuckoo Siva's spotless white Adidas trainers.

Cuckoo Siva pulls him to his feet, taps him on his head and points to a chair.

'Sir, sir, you saved my life.' Jinesena grabs Cuckoo Siva's hand in both of his and lowers his head to kiss it.

Cuckoo Siva looks around the room, until a policeman pulls Jinesena away and sits him down again. Wiping his hands on a policeman's back, Cuckoo Siva says, 'You jumped in, risking your own life to save that boy.'

'Ah, so I did save him? Jinesena smiles and stands up straight. 'I have made something of my life after all. I am a hero. I am a hero, hero, hero.'

'No, actually you dragged him down further.'

'Oh.'

'But the point is, you tried.' Cuckoo Siva grabs Jinesena's hand and kisses it. 'That boy, Madu, is my son. My slightly errant son, who is trying to come to terms with my rocky relationship with his mother. It's one of those things, you know. Neither parent wants to punish him because we need him on our respective side. So he gets away with murder. He was smoking a joint on the rocks when this happened. He doesn't know this but my men are always watching him. They called me and I came in time to see him fall in the sea, but I thought, you know what, let's leave him to suffer a bit. Learn a lesson. A nineteen-year-old boy and still not a man.'

'So he wasn't going to drown?'

'No.' Cuckoo Siva ambles towards the window and looks out. 'But you weren't to know that. Can you swim?'

'Some say I can,' Jinesena says.

'Are those people right?' Cuckoo Siva asks.

'Not as such.'

'Yes, it looked that way. But the point is you tried. Do you have children?'

'One boy,' Jinesena says. 'Name is Nalaka.'

'He must be very proud of you. Your children should always be your number one priority, wouldn't you say?'

'I would.'

'I hear you stole a bike.'

'Not really, sir.'

'I am dead against any form of crime.'

'Sir, the shop owner put up the price he had agreed on. I left him money.'

'I've heard the whole story, and what he did is also a crime.' Cuckoo Siva clicks his fingers and one of his men brings the bike in. 'Is this it?'

'You found it?' Jinesena is beaming.

Cuckoo Siva mounts the bike and when he sits on the saddle, his knees almost touch the floor. 'You got this for your son?'

Jinesena begins to cry. He wipes tears out of his eyes and nods.

'When I had no money,' Cuckoo Siva says, 'like you, I would have done anything to get things for my son even if I had to beg, steal and borrow.'

Jinesena nods. 'Sir, I didn't think I was stealing.'

'But you begged from Monsoon Lodge members. Borrowed too?'

'Yes, sir.'

'But when you got away with the bike, you risked losing it all to save my boy. Why?'

'Because, sir, I imagined that it was my boy. I hope someone would risk their life to save him too.'

'Exactly.' Cuckoo Siva bends down and hugs Jinesena so tight there is no air left in him. He rises to his feet and clicks his fingers again and his men remove the bike from the office. 'But I can't let you give him this bicycle.'

'But, sir, I have cancer and not a long time to live so –'

'Stop, stop.' Cuckoo Siva raises a hand. 'No more lying, please.'

'Sir, Nalaka is expecting that bike,' Jinesena says.

'I'm sure he's expecting something better.'

'We are simple people.'

'But a father is his son's hero. You have to live up to that.' Cuckoo Siva looks down at his phone. 'I have been researching this and I think the most suitable bike would be an Islabike Cnoc. It is the lightest kid's bike on the market, and this makes it easier to manoeuvre and control. I take it Nalaka has never ridden a bike before?'

'No, sir.'

'So he may as well start with the best.' Cuckoo Siva nods to his men who bring in another bike, painted in police colours with a basket and lights. 'When I was teaching Mr Krishan a lesson or two, he told me exactly what you were after. Gave this for free. Even painted it himself.'

Jinesena holds his head. His body feels tingly. The most amazing feeling ever.

'Nalaka's on his way here.' Cuckoo Siva clicks his fingers one more time and everyone else leaves the office. 'Get behind the desk.'

Looking around the room, Jinesena points at himself. 'Me?'

'Yes, you. The OIC offered you his uniform, but Nalaka will wonder why you left home wearing this.' Cuckoo Siva chucks Jinesena his mauve Monsoon Lodge beret. 'If he asks, just say you have a special uniform because you're the officer-in-charge. The OIC.'

Jinesena sits behind the desk. 'But he has a friend, whose father –'

'Dilshan? Don't worry about what he says.' Cuckoo Siva strides to the door. 'I've done some things in my life I'm not proud of. I hear the whispers wherever I go. But the thing is, it doesn't bother me what others think. All that bothers me is what my son thinks of me. Is he proud to tell people I am his father? Does he think I am a good person? That's all that matters. I judge people well, and Mr Jinesena, you are a great father.'

'That means a lot to me, sir.'

'Even though, it seems you may be a hopeless employee.'

'That means a bit less.'

Cuckoo Siva laughs. 'Deal?'

'Sir, please don't misunderstand.' Jinesena stands up and moves away from the desk. 'What you have offered is the kindest thing. But I am not sure I can accept.'

'Say again?' Cuckoo Siva asks.

'You see, I know now that I must be honest with my son.'

Nalaka sees his father outside Kollupitiya police station with a bike he knows is meant for him. He has never seen anything so amazing in his life, and all he can do is cry. Cry, that is, and stroke the handlebar, smell the tyres, try the bell. This is a million dreams come true.

'Mine?' he asks his father.

'Yours,' Jinesena says. 'But son, there's something I have to tell you.'

'About the bike?'

'About me.' Jinesena takes off his hat, bends down and shows it to his son. 'This says Monsoon Lodge Senior Security Guard. I'm sorry, I know you wanted to believe I'm a policeman, but ...'

'I know, Thathi.'

'What?'

'I thought you wanted me to play along so I did.' Nalaka climbs on the bike. 'You're my father that's all I need to know.'

'So you always knew I was a guard?'

'Of course, Thathi.' Nalaka rings the bell. 'I worried

so much about you because you were telling me such ridiculous lies. I thought you had become like Susil Uncle, a lovable idiot.'

Devil Mask Tattoo

ANJALI AND RAJIV are buck naked when both their phones beep thrice at exactly the same time. It is six in the morning, and the sun is just beginning to rise above the long line of bamboo trees in Rajiv's garden. Anjali picks her phone up first, opening a message from the police that reads as follows:

This is an automated message sent to everyone on Sri Lankan cellular networks: The sole witness in the Sky City Killings has come out of her coma and recalls a devil mask tattoo on the upper chest of the killer. Please be vigilant and contact the police immediately if you have any information.

Anjali is consumed by fear as she reads the same message in Sinhala and Tamil. She looks over at Rajiv who has his eyes closed. They have been naked together for over six hours so they know everything about each other's bodies, down to smells, errant hairs, bruises and tattoos.

Both their phones beep again. This time Anjali finds an MMS from the police with a familiar generic image of a devil mask – predominantly red and black, bulging eyes, long teeth, and cobras for hair.

When Anjali looks to her right, Rajiv is reading the messages. He looks over her shoulder and when he realizes she has also seen these messages, he drops his phone and pulls an antique hand axe off his wall.

Rajiv becomes the hunter, Anjali the hunted.

The Sky City killings has become the most high-profile unsolved murder case in Sri Lanka since an English sports journalist and a school cricket coach were discovered hanging from a street lamp in 2006. In the penthouse of Colombo's tallest building, a naked woman and man were discovered dead in what looked to be either a crime of passion, or a sex game gone wrong. Another person – the dead man's maid who had probably arrived for her shift – was found at the door of the bathroom with near-fatal head injuries from being bludgeoned with a shower head.

Anjali had met Rajiv at Silk Nightclub the night before they received the text messages that sparked off the hunt. She recognized him from the newspapers; he had been interviewed by the police because he was rumoured to have had a recent fling with the female victim of the Sky City killings. When Anjali approached him at the bar, he looked right through her. His eyes were like cloudy marbles, darting all over the place. Maybe it was the drink, maybe it was the drugs, or maybe it was that, as Anjali would find out, his wife had left him.

Anjali knew all about such pain. The love of her life, her high-school sweetheart, had refused to marry her. His reason? Her lack of privacy, her sharing of personal stories on Facebook, and her open and proud enjoyment of sex. Now he is married to a sari-wearing, spatula-wielding, over-educated Sinhalese Buddhist lady with a Kandyan name. Anjali still parties and drinks to forget him. That is how she ended up at Silk Nightclub.

Rajiv wore tight clothes, and had purposely messy hair and a trimmed beard. Anjali needed to see him naked and that's what she was going to do. She had never been restricted by her family's conservatism. If she fancied someone she slept with them.

It took two drinks and a dance to get Rajiv outside. He had rock-star parking for his BMW R 1200 R Exclusive motorcycle metres from the front entrance. Fully black, and with sharp lines, it looked like something Batman would be happy to show off. Anjali had always been a biker lady; brought up by a stepfather who liked her more than he liked her mother, she had spent hours of her youth working on his bikes with him.

Rajiv suggested Anjali ride the bike, with him at the back. He passed her one of his two helmets, which looked like something the Nazis used to wear. When she put it on, it just covered the top of her head, so her highlighted blonde hair was loose below it. They zoomed up and down Marine Drive, the spitting sea splashing into their uncovered faces.

'With the wind in my eyes,' Rajiv said, as they hit 100 mph, 'I can't see anything.'

Cranking up the speed further, Anjali said, 'Neither can I.'

When they got to his place, Anjali and Rajiv drank champagne on his cantilevered wooden deck, overlooking a lake and bird sanctuary which they could just about make out under the half moon. It began to beat down with rain so they moved into the sitting room which was open and airy, enclosed only by retractable metal criss-cross gates. Anjali was impressed by Rajiv's taste in art, if indeed it was his and not his ex-wife's. The standout piece was a fifteen-foot coal sketch of a rat that was as disturbing as it was oddly powerful. To its right, an open rock staircase led up to the bedrooms. Past that, and still part of the living room, a fish pond so big it looked like a hotel swimming pool. The roof above it was open, so rain pelted down with such noise Anjali could not hear a word Rajiv said.

Instead she lunged at him. Her tongue down his throat, her hand on his thigh, moving up. Soon they were upstairs. They found themselves next on the balcony, making love under the stars as the rain evaporated off the rock steps around them. He made all the right noises and all the right moves but never smiled. After the second time, they fell asleep together, waking soon after for one more session. Because Rajiv prohibited smoking in his bedroom (his ex-wife's rule) they moved into the TV room to light up, their free hands locked together.

That was then, before any mention of a killer with a devil mask tattoo.

The early-morning text messages changed everything, as light began to snake in upstairs. Now when Anjali sees Rajiv clutching the hand axe, she kicks open the double doors of the TV room and sprints down the corridor. She remembers that the bathroom can be locked because earlier she almost got stuck in there when she went for a mid-sex clean-up. She slams the door shut and bolts it at the top and bottom.

Rajiv is punching his fists against the door shouting something she cannot make out over the beating of the tropical rain. Her heart is pumping because she could tell from Rajiv's eyes that he had lost it. There is no way he will let her escape. She does not feel safe in the bathroom but she knows she has a few minutes at least. Ideally she needs to call for help but her phone is in the bedroom and when she looks out the window all she can see is a lake. She needs a weapon, and the best she can do is break off the hand shower next to the loo, but what will she achieve with that? She vomits into a bowl by the sink and continues gagging once she has done so.

There is a bang against the door and Anjali jumps back. With the second hit, she sees the blade of the axe. She throws the bucket of vomit at the newly formed hole in the door, then climbs in and out of the cement bathtub and up to the window. Looking below she sees a ledge which runs the length of the upper floor. Rajiv calls this feature the eyebrow of the house, there to protect the open spaces below from getting too wet. The bathroom door crashes open, but now Anjali is on the ledge and running to the master balcony at the far end of the upper floor. She slips on the way, her legs hanging off the ledge but she pulls herself up. With her jaws clenched, she charges for the balcony and jumps to reach its walls, but then she feels Rajiv's fingers around her wrists, before she manages to wiggle her soaking and slippery arms free. She falls back on the ledge, returning to her feet just before Rajiv hurls the axe at her. The butt of the blade catches the back of her ankle, drawing blood.

Anjali hops to the other side of the upper floor. The eyebrow ledge curves round the house so she aims for another balcony but Rajiv gets there before she does and points a rifle at her and fires. The silent shot hits her in the left breast and hurts like hell, but doesn't penetrate. It must be an airgun pellet, she thinks. He lifts the rifle to his shoulder again and takes aim as she retreats. The pellet strikes her between the bare cheeks of her backside, making her drop to her knees, but rather than giving him the chance to hit her naked flesh a third time, she gets back up and jumps into the fish pond below. Her fall is cushioned not just by water, but also by two-foot-long orange and black fish, which her feet press into at the bottom of the pond before they splash away. She wades through the water on her hands and knees, the rain hammering onto her back like needles. To her left she sees Rajiv, still naked, balls bouncing, running down the stairs. He slips at the bottom and while he is on his arse, Anjali decides to get out of the pond and makes a run for the far end of the sitting room. She gets there before he returns to his feet. He makes little effort to do so in any hurry because, as she finds out, he must have known the retractable crisscross gate is locked.

She shakes the gate so much it feels like it will give way but it bounces back up each time. The grass, the trees, the tree house, the lake, the rain, the road are in her view but she can't get to them because of the bloody gate. She shakes it again and it rattles, it bends, it snaps, but it doesn't open. Rajiv is right behind her. She turns to look at him. They are dead still, the only movement is the pond water dripping down her legs.

Anjali smiles, as if to say, *Come on, what's with the chase? We just made love three times.* 'Just let me go, please,' she says.

Rajiv's facial expressions are locked in a scowl and he says nothing. Behind him, above the fish pond, the rain stops and in a moment the sun shoots out, lighting up the sitting room. Now, with the sun reflecting off the water and between the gap in her legs, Anjali wonders whether she can distract him enough to be able to fight him. She knows he is strong. He demonstrated that the night before. She knows she can't run away from him for long. She looks for a weakness but instead she sees the red of his eyes. The tensing of his jaw. She knows this is her or him. They can't both survive.

Taking in deep breaths she starts to believe that this is the end. The day she pays for her past. The day her childhood sweetheart celebrates the death of his slut ex-bird. Yet, she can't give up. She has to keep fighting. The world has always been against her but has never beaten her.

She tries to scream loud enough for the closest neighbours to hear but she no longer has the lungs for it and her throat is sandpaper dry. Her heart is pounding too fast, drumming against her ribs. Her breathing is raspy, inconsistent.

'Let's talk,' she says to Rajiv, but he snarls, almost growls and Anjali knows that he will win unless she is very clever about this.

She takes deep breaths and looks around. Anjali and Rajiv circle each other, like sumo wrestlers. He inches in a bit, she inches out a bit. She makes one final dash upstairs, knowing that the only way she can get out of the house is by jumping off the master bedroom balcony. Rajiv follows her up, albeit at his own pace. She hears him behind her so she jumps and, on landing, she falls on her back, clutching at her ankle. Rajiv looks over the balcony, then backs away. Anjali assumes he must be coming down the stairs.

She gets back onto one foot and hops towards the tree house. She hears his footsteps – he is now in flip-flops – as he gains on her with too much speed for her liking.

She cannot stay on one foot and drops back down to the wet grass and, as she turns, her nudity is obscured by mud. Above her, he lifts a spade and whacks at her. She turns just in time to take the blow on her shoulder rather than her face, but her whole body is jarred and left in astonishing pain.

The game is up, she thinks. *He is going to kill me. One last chance.* Before he lifts the spade above his head she is on her knees diving at him, teeth first, growling, hungry. She takes a large chunk of his right calf in her mouth and he screams and drops the spade.

She is back on her feet, the weight on her good leg as she kicks at his bushy testicles. He drops to his knees, tripping her with his outstretched arm as she tries to run past him. He gets on her back hammering her with his fists, but she is muddy and just about strong enough to slip away. She gets to the spade and swings it down at him. He lifts his arms to block the blow, but then he drops them in pain and she has a free shot at his face. She connects with a golfer's timing and he falls to the floor, face down in the mud, almost unconscious.

Anjali runs to the gate but when she sees a hose pipe she stops for a second. It is not safe to leave Rajiv as he is. She returns to him and wraps the blue hose pipe round his neck and starts tightening it. He wakes briefly to slap his hands against the mud, splattering her in the process.

Then he is dead.

Anjali goes back into the house, through the now unlocked retractable metal gates. She climbs the stairs to have a shower, putting her black party clothes back on, before finding something to wrap around her ankle wound. While she applies make-up, she hears the bell ring. She looks at the CCTV screen. At the front gate stands a maid arriving for her shift and through the letterbox she sees Rajiv's naked dead body and she screams, before retreating down the street.

Limping down the stairs, Anjali hitches up her black jeans before getting on the BMW Batman-like motorbike. She puts on the Nazi-style helmet and presses a red switch on the wall in the garage. The roller-gate rises. There is a police siren in the distance. Anjali revs the engine and is off, safe in the knowledge that Rajiv will never be able to tell anyone that she has a devil mask tattoo just above her right breast.

Tuk Tuk Bang

TWO YEARS AFTER a debt collector broke his leg, Akila Balige is back in the gym running ten kilometres in under an hour. He follows this up with a session with his trainer, Bicep Badula, focusing on core strength to compensate for the power he lost in his legs. He needs to exercise every day to feel a sense of the self-worth he all but lost when his wife left him because he was travelling the world for an ungrateful government. After a shower, he sits at the gym cafe having a weight-gainer shake, while he stalks his wife on social media. It hurts him when he sees her in photographs with other men, but not as much as the fear of Ranita, his six-year-old daughter, calling someone else Thathi – that word is really important to him.

Having spent six months away from home spying on disgruntled and politically active members of the diaspora, all Balige has to show for it is a red Toyota Landcruiser with an official government-issue VIP sticker. Balige may be small, but that sticker tells people he's better than them, even if it didn't sway things for his marriage.

Balige was educated at Isthuthi College and Warwick University, the latter paid for with hush money by a man named Chinthika Balasuriya who refuses to acknowledge that he is his father. Now Balasuriya languishes in a prison hospital with a fictitious ailment that will keep him out of a cell for as long as he can bribe the right people. He had hoodwinked a nation, collecting funds from anyone who believed in his 30% annual returns, including politicians, half the national cricket team, charities and the Church of Conrad Cecil. Somehow he is still alive, and somehow he still denies two things most vehemently – that he ran a Ponzi scheme and that Akila Balige is his son from a mother who worked as his secretary at the time.

Balige had tried to climb the hierarchy of the Sri Lankan government, trying to mimic his father's apparent success and power. Yet, behind the closed doors of government offices, he is being punished for his father's misdemeanours. Why, they wonder, will Balige not stop making this outlandish claim that he is the son of the most hated man in the country? The answer is simple: he wants what others take for granted – someone to call Thathi.

At the best of times Balige has so much rage bubbling inside him. That was kept in check by a ten-day Vipassana meditation course, in which he found it easy to stick to the vow of silence because he didn't want to speak to anyone anyway. His gym sessions help too, but he is as painfully lonely as any man who has lost family life would be. Even though he is at his lowest point emotionally, everything about his life is disciplined and impeccably planned, but the one place he can't be in control is on Colombo roads. He often thinks that if he had a gun he would use it on tuktuk drivers who weave in and out of speeding cars as if it's a game; or on the bus drivers who race each other for fares, regardless of oncoming traffic.

Now, with sweat in his eyes, Balige tries to turn right onto Japan Sri Lanka Friendship Road, but hits a freshly painted green tuktuk in the process. He takes a deep breath and closes his eyes. He could go one of two ways here: release all his rage around his father, his wife, his government and not worry about the consequences, or try to become a better person. He rubs his temples and looks across the lake towards Parliament, a serene, tropical building inside which uneducated politicians have irrelevant arguments. He decides he is going to be the better man and not bother getting compensation from the tuktuk driver even though it was his fault. That would involve making a police entry which would ruin his meticulous plans for the rest of the day. He gets out, ignoring the other driver's extended hand, and checks the damage to his jeep. The plastic rim above his tyres has been dislodged and some of the jeep's red paint has been scratched off, but that is all.

To assert his control over the situation, Balige marches over to the tuktuk driver, looking him up and down. The tuktuk driver is an older gentleman, possibly in his sixties. There is something very cool and film-star-like about him. Maybe it is his slicked-back silver hair, or his suspiciously perfect teeth or his energized skin. He wears a striped sarong and a white shirt which are both immaculately laundered and ironed. Balige can't help but notice that he looks considerably more distinguished than his own father, the slobbering fat wreck wolfing down fast food in prison. 'You guys need to start sticking to road rules just like the rest of us,' Balige says.

'Us guys?' the tuktuk driver looks around at the gathering onlookers. 'You mean poor people?'

'Taxi drivers,' Balige says. 'I know you're in a race to catch more fares, but, you know ...' He looks at his watch. 'Look, I'm in a hurry, let's settle this quickly.' He reaches out his hand.

The tuktuk driver takes it in both of his, grins, bows a little and says, 'I am Wijayanandan of Hokandara South.'

Ignoring the chance to offer his own name, Balige points to the tuktuk. 'Let's check the damage.'

The first thing Balige notices are the photographs that plaster the tuktuk's interiors – the old man with kids of various ages on his lap. Wijayanandan notices him looking and says, 'Eight grandchildren. Ages two to fourteen.' He laughs for no apparent reason. 'I take passengers to help with their expenses.'

Balige has pictures like this with his daughter but not with his father. Here is a man who is a shockingly bad driver, but a good father and grandfather. This is becoming pretty open and shut. Once Wijayanandan apologizes, Balige will tap him on the back and give him the good news that he will not charge him anything for the damage to his jeep. In fact, he will even offer to pay for the tuktuk's repairs.

By now, a crowd has begun to take shape around the accident. Hell, any accident is fun, but when you get one between a tuktuk and a VIP car, you have all the ingredients for a blockbuster argument. So there are people trying to help, people offering advice, people plain bored and looking for some excitement. Each of them asks if Balige and Wijayanandan are okay, and a few offer water and cigarettes.

They follow Balige as he examines the tuktuk's damage, which is barely noticeable. There are a few scratches and dents and a little bit of the jeep's red paint above the front wheel. 'Maybe this will cost less than five thousand?' Balige asks.

'Not sure, sir,' Wijayanandan says. 'I think if you give me fifteen thousand I can pay for my repairs without having to report your mistake to the police.'

Balige bends forward, closes his eyes and lights a cigarette. This is what he does when the rage takes over. Sometimes it works, sometimes it doesn't. He can feel the blood flooding his head, as he puffs out his cheeks and takes big drags of smoke. He knows there is a massive rich–poor divide in this country but he hates this sense of entitlement. This notion that the rich should throw money at the poor even when the latter is at fault. 'Why should I give you any money?'

Wijayanandan laughs. There's nothing that bothers Balige more than when people laugh or smile after having done something wrong. Wijayanandan points at the damage to his tuktuk. 'Because ...'

'You should be giving me money, not the other way round.'

The crowd laughs and then turns, like in a tennis match, to look at Wijayanandan, waiting for his response.

Wijayanandan stops laughing as if he has suddenly realized that Balige isn't joking. 'Sir, please don't misunderstand, but you hit my tuk,' he says, his arms by his sides.

More laughter from the crowd, but now accompanied by some shushes. Various members of the audience begin to appreciate that things could become more dramatic.

Balige points to where they had crashed. 'But you were overtaking me on the inside while I was turning.'

'Yes, sir. Then you hit me,' he says again.

'I saw that,' says one of the onlookers.

'Thank God,' Balige says. 'What did you see?'

'You hit his tuk,' the man says and the others nod.

'But ...' Balige grunts and picks out the one guy in the crowd who looks like he might be educated. 'Can you explain to them that you can't overtake someone on the inside when they are turning?'

'But there was space,' the man says. 'Yet you hit him.'

Balige desperately wants to pay this tuktuk driver and be done with it, but that would be like his father paying for his university just to shut him up. Still, he knows he has to be the bigger person so he takes in a deep breath. It is not like he will ever see this man again, so why must he prove he is right to him? 'Fine. You need to read the driving laws and maybe do your test again.' Balige looks towards the crowd. 'Seems like you all do. But look, as an act of kindness ...' He holds five thousand rupees and his business card out for Wijayanandan. 'If it costs more, come to me with the receipts and I'll pay.'

Wijayanandan collects the money in his right hand, while his left hand supports his wrist. Balige appreciates this sign of respect as he watches the tuktuk driver kiss the money and then bow as he backs away.

Balige is proud of himself. Maybe he is coming to terms with all that is wrong in his life, and besides, it's not the tuktuk driver's fault that he is an idiot.

'Sir,' Wijayanandan says, 'you are good man. Very good man. May the blessings of the triple gem always be with you.'

'And the force with you.' Balige smiles and lifts his hands up in prayer. 'Look after your grandkids.'

Wijayanandan gets into his tuktuk, and lifts up the lever to get the engine running. 'Sir, rich people do not normally admit they are wrong to poor people like me.' He points at the sticker on Balige's jeep. 'Especially VIPs.'

'I wasn't wrong. It was your fault.'

Wijayanandan laughs. 'Maybe next time you can use your side mirror, then no accident.' Wijayanandan points to the photos of his grandkids. 'There are a lot of kids on the road these days, so better to drive carefully.'

By now his tuktuk engine is sputtering as he leans out to see if he can get back onto the main road.

Balige knows he should let this go. He leans back against the jeep's bumper and punches his own thighs. He plans to take ten deep breaths through his nose and into his chest, but he only gets to five when he hears someone laughing. It could be anyone but Balige assumes they are laughing at him. Something snaps. It is like a switch, because at that very moment he feels like Wijayanandan is mocking him. He charges towards the tuktuk, but is held back by four men. 'Do you know who I am?' he shouts.

Cowering with his hands up, Wijayanandan says, 'Sir, sir, take your money back, sir please.' He throws it towards him and a split second later he joins traffic, almost colliding with a family on a motorcycle.

Balige shoves away the men holding him, and takes a few more deep breaths. He slaps out the new creases in his clothes and gets into his jeep. Whacking the steering wheel with his palms, Balige turns the key and floors the accelerator, screeching off across the road. He knows he has to find the old bastard to teach him a lesson. This proves harder than he expected because there are so many green tuktuks on the road, and also his vision is a little clouded by the sweat dripping from his brow. He tries to reason with himself. *Let it go. Be the bigger man*, but he has to make Wijayanandan know it was his fault even if it means dragging him home and tying him to a chair while he teaches him the laws of the roads. While he teaches him about respect.

He catches up with Wijayanandan as he turns towards the new army camp construction site. Beeping his horn continuously, Balige needs to get in front of the tuktuk but the other side of the road is chock-a-block with cars. He flashes his lights and follows the tuktuk across a narrow, pot-holed road that bisects a lake. Wijayanandan is doing all he can to get away, swerving down smaller and smaller roads. He looks out the side of his tuktuk, from time to time, with blind fear in his eyes.

Driving side by side, they force a family of black wild boar to wobble off the road. Balige rolls down his window to shout at Wijayanandan as they speed down Kanatte Road, but he is blocked by a pile of rocks left in the middle of the road by a construction site. So he has ground to make up on Wijayanandan, and despite hearing police sirens, he floors the accelerator.

But then he has to hit the brakes because a woman on a massive black motorbike, her highlighted hair cascading through a Nazi-looking war helmet, crashes against the green tuktuk. The bike then skids across the road, and in order to avoid it Balige swerves to the left and almost takes out a muscular woman in a fluorescent yellow tank top. He drives over something and hears a dog squeal. He stops next to the overturned tuktuk and when he opens his door, the muscular lady points at him and shouts out, 'Stop that man, stop that man.'

A police car zooms past and stops by the bike. Now a silver Audi slows down by the dead dog and the muscular lady.

Suffering light burns from his seatbelt and a jarred knee, Balige hobbles out of his jeep and limps towards the tuktuk. Wijayanandan's eyes are wide open, but they are lifeless. Balige doubles up and gags, then he sees those pictures of Wijayanandan's grandchildren, as if they too are looking at him. Asking him where their grandfather is; their seeya.

Balige thinks of Ranita, the daughter he did not make time for because he was too busy trying to become a VIP. If he walks away right now, he realizes he has a chance to reconnect with her. To make amends. Maybe he can even prove to his wife that he is worthy of their love. Maybe he can get over this need for acceptance from his father, but all he can do for Wijayanandan is slip twenty thousand rupees in his pocket and hope his family will find it.

A man gets out of the silver Audi down the road and jogs towards the dead lady on the motorbike. Balige can help as well, but then he might be culpable for the accident, so instead he gets in his red jeep and drives away, knowing he will deny the truth and in so doing he will finally become like his father.

CHHIMI TENDUF-LA

My Fair & Lovely Lady

PASINDU AMARASINGHE HATED his mother coming to his school cricket matches because he didn't want the other students to discover how poor he was. Ammi knew this so she would turn up dressed like Eliza Doolittle. She wore white gloves and carried an umbrella with frills that she stitched herself using old napkins. She also made sandwiches for all the other parents and kids, which people were kind enough to eat even though they were filled with rubbery cuts of meat. Pasindu hated those sandwiches because they were embarrassing and cost the kind of money to make that Ammi didn't have. She used to work two jobs, earning just enough to pay the rent for their one-room annex to a modest man's house, but not enough to be feeding the elite of Colombo.

When Pasindu got a scholarship to a private school, Ammi started using Fair & Lovely whitening cream because she noticed all the other mothers were not as dark as she was. The first time she came to watch Pasindu play she wore a sari – it was the same sari she had worn for her wedding; white with gold embroidery. One player from an opposing team, who spoke with an Australian accent, sledged Pasindu by telling him his mother looked like a meringue. Another called her an espresso – short and black.

Ammi knew almost a hundred words in English at the time, but she had the confidence to use only about four in public. If she asked one of the other parents something in Sinhala, they would reply very slowly in English. She would smile, wobble her head and then look to Pasindu for a translation which he would be too embarrassed to offer. To fill the ensuing silence, Ammi would offer everyone a 'cup of chino' which was just Nescafe with lots of powdered milk.

The first day she came dressed as Eliza Doolittle, Pasindu hid in the team's dressing room. He wanted to curl up into a ball and disappear into the ground. He knew everyone would be laughing at them, saying they were a 'jungo' family trying to fit in. Yet, worse than anything else was when Ammi started giving presents to the other players. She would gift stickers and stationery, badges and sometimes even tubes of toothpaste. Things she valued, but these were thirteen-year-old rich kids. Unfortunately, they were trained to be polite so they always said they loved the presents which only encouraged her more.

Pasindu's rival at school, when he first joined, was a tough kid called Manjula Wijeratne. His on-the-pitch talents matched Pasindu's but he had no scholarship because he was too rich to need one. Pasindu, and all the other kids, envied him. Even though he was barely a teen, he used to rock up to matches on a moped, painted in black with a gold lightning sticker on either side. He always wore an unzipped tracksuit jacket with nothing underneath it, except for his washboard abs and carved-out pecs. His parents never embarrassed him by coming to watch him play. Instead they treated him as an adult, so much so that he had his own keys to their house and never had to ask permission to go out.

Pasindu was intimidated by Manjula. He wanted to be his friend – hell he wanted to be his best friend – but because he idolized him so much he was often mute in his presence. When they changed together before a match, Manjula would ask lots of questions and Pasindu would just nod or give one-word answers.

All the girls loved Manjula because he had the confidence to go with the freedom he enjoyed. On the other hand, Pasindu found it hard to look a girl in the eye and even if he could he wouldn't dare because Ammi would always turn up to highlight, in Sinhala, her son's virtues.

'Did you know my son can make string hoppers? Did you know he loves to sing and dance? Did you know he has a fast metabolism? Would you believe he has two head baths a day?'

Or addressing Pasindu in front of a girl: 'Putha, why did you not tell me you had such a beautiful girlfriend?'

'Ammi, we have only just met.'

'That may be the case, but a mother can always tell. She loves you too.'

Worse than anything else, she would sometimes invite girls home, and Pasindu never wanted anyone to see where they lived. When queen bee Iresha Guruge visited, he was excited to be part of the in-crowd but utterly ashamed at the same time.

Pasindu and Ammi did all they could to make their room look presentable but that was tricky because most of their possessions were hand-me-downs and rejects. Iresha smiled as best she could and remained stoically polite at all times, but she was not comfortable conversing in Sinhala.

Pasindu felt that to Iresha this was like social work; visiting the disadvantaged. She struggled to drink the tea with four sugars and condensed milk that Ammi made especially for her and she seemed reluctant to sit on any of the wobbly chairs. When she asked to use the phone, they had to direct her to their landlord's house. Less than fifteen minutes later, Manjula arrived on his moped to pick her up. It did not escape Pasindu's notice that the first time Iresha truly smiled was when she was leaving.

Pasindu tried to pretend that he was cool with this. He didn't want Ammi to fawn over him, but she did anyway whilst wiping away her own tears.

'I'm so sorry, putha. You would be the perfect catch, if only your mother could provide for you.'

She hugged him tight, but Pasindu's arms hung limply by his side. When he thought of going to school the next day, his stomach felt strange. He feared losing Iresha to a better boy and he couldn't help remembering how much happier he was back at his village school.

The day before the Middle School Inter-international cricket final, the coach told the players that the Sri Lankan under-fourteen squad was to be picked and three members of the team were in line for selection. Ammi was so excited that she couldn't sleep. She paced up and down all night, rummaging around her son's kit, making sure everything was clean.

Ammi turned up for the match with a box of coloured pencils which she shared amongst the players before they warmed up. She allocated the colours according to how she saw each player, and, of course, she ended up giving her son the pink one. Pasindu chucked the pencil in the bin in front of everyone. He knew he would become a laughing stock and, at that moment, he hated Ammi and never wanted to speak to her again. He approached the other boys hoping there would be some sort of macho respect for defying his mother, but Manjula wouldn't make eye contact and turned away.

Pasindu scored 87 violent runs that day. He tried to hit pretty much every ball out of the ground and it came off because his thoughts were so uncluttered. He didn't care if he failed; all he wanted was to blow off steam. As it turned out it was too late. The under-fourteen national team had already been picked and it was announced that Manjula was in, as was Ranjith, the leg-spinner, but Pasindu wasn't. Ammi tried to hug her son in front of everyone else, but he nudged her away and sprinted over to the far end of Shalika Grounds where an old double-decker bus was standing in as the scoreboard. He climbed up the stairs to the top level and sobbed away, losing breath, tears merging with sweat in their journey down his face. All the emotions of the last few years. Their living conditions. Their shame. How Ammi had essentially kicked his father and the little money he had out of their lives, just because he would occasionally turn abusive when drunk. Pasindu did not envy the other students their wealth; he envied them their fathers. Since his had left and because Ammi was too damn stupid to hold down a well-paying job, he decided, there and then, that as soon as he graduated a few years later, he would move out and fend for himself.

When his tears dried up, he looked out the window of the bus and watched Ranjith's parents ruffle his hair and hug most of the air out of him. Manjula, though, as cool as they came, put on his sunglasses and got on his moped. He was about to ride off when Ammi went chasing after him. She hugged him and pulled him to the grass so he would sit next to her. They talked for what seemed to be at least twenty minutes, and then they hugged again.

After everyone had left, Pasindu shooed Ammi away and went back to the dressing room. As annoying as she was, because she tried so hard, Pasindu almost cried again when he saw most of the pencils she had given out, lying on the muddy floor. He was pretty sure she would have skipped meals to be able to buy them. He tried to keep her out of the dressing room but it was virtually impossible to keep her out of anything. She pretended that she didn't see the pencils but Pasindu knew she had because she didn't speak all the way home – this had never happened before.

A few days later Pasindu found the pencils back in the box on the shelf above Ammi's bed. Some were broken, some were barely touched. He looked at the picture on the box and worked out that only the blue and the pink pencils were missing.

By the time Pasindu entered grade 12, his mother was doing well enough to afford a two-bedroom house, so she couldn't understand why he wanted to move out so soon after he graduated. Ammi tried to visit him every day but he always said he was too tired. They spent the whole of every Sunday together, cooking his curries for the week and playing Scrabble. Since she had more time on her hands, she had learnt a little more English. This tradition continued until she died of breast cancer in July 2016. Pasindu was twenty-three years old.

Between late 2014 and early 2016, Manjula Wijeratne had established himself as one of the five best young batsmen in the world, along with Virat Kohli, Joe Root, Kane Williamson and Steve Smith. Manjula had not talked to anyone from the school since he left five years earlier. Everyone claimed that he had got too big for his boots, but Pasindu wondered if it was because he was hurt by what happened at Graduation Ball. Either way, Pasindu was very touched that he came to Ammi's funeral. He looked as sharp as he did in all the billboards around town; slicked-back hair, tight bicep-grabbing clothes, thousand-dollar sunglasses and a designer bag over his shoulder. As usual, Pasindu thought, Manjula somehow managed to steal the limelight at the wrong time. But then, he just left without even offering his condolences.

Pasindu went through the motions saying the right things to the wrong people, ninety per cent of whom had never met Ammi. Pretty much anyone Pasindu had ever talked to came to say goodbye to this lady to whom they had never said hello. As the last of the mourners joined the line at the bus stop outside, Pasindu sat alone waiting for Ammi's ashes. He heard footsteps – wooden-soled expensive shoes – and looked up.

'May I?' Manjula asked, pointing to the next step down.

Pasindu nodded and put a hand out to him, but he ignored it and hugged him instead. 'I remember your mother in her white gloves and –'

'Umbrella,' Pasindu said. 'How embarrassing.'

'And her sandwiches,' Manjula said.

'A bit crap, right?'

'Disgusting.' He laughed. 'But I always ate them. Pretty much the only homemade food I've ever eaten.'

'You must think homemade food is overrated.'

'Massively,' Manjula said. 'You hated your mum coming to matches, didn't you?'

'The bane of my existence.'

Manjula put a hand on Pasindu's shoulder. 'You know, the first match my mother came to was only when I was already quite famous. She figured she could watch me and be photographed for *Hi* at the same time.'

'And give everyone a pencil sharpener?'

Manjula laughed in the way that charmed millions around the world. 'Your mother loved to give gifts, no?' He lifted an arm in the air. 'If I ever scored a fifty I would raise my bat and look for your mother in the crowd because she was always clapping the loudest. The other players used to raise their bats to their parents, but mine weren't there and she was the only one who noticed that.'

Pasindu sensed that this was a moment for reflection so remained silent for as long as he could. Then his curiosity got the better of him. 'I have to ask you.' He closed his eyes and grinned. 'What did she say to you that day you got selected for the under-fourteens?'

'Something I thought was batshit crazy, but it didn't matter. I knew she was with me. On my side. She gave me some of the worst advice I have ever heard, but she laboured over it. It meant something, to her at least.'

Manjula turned away and covered his eyes and as he did, a man handed a clay pot full of Ammi's ashes to Pasindu.

'See,' Pasindu smiled, 'even now she pops up at the wrong time.'

'You're a cruel bastard.' Manjula laughed. 'You know, when we got close to beating India in the test series, I rented a massive box for the decider. Somehow your mother got in there one of the days and she found my fiancée.'

'You're engaged?' Pasindu asked, surprised that it bothered him to hear this.

Manjula flashed his ring. 'Your mother left a brand new bat for me.' Manjula laughed, rubbing his eyes. 'I have hundreds of bats, but she wasn't to know that. She told my fiancée she had come every day of the match but wouldn't make it on Sunday as that was the one day she got to see you.'

Pasindu had to hold his breath for a second. 'She meant well I guess.'

'Very.' Manjula lifted the flap on his bag and pulled out a small box which he handed to Pasindu. 'I think you may appreciate this more now.'

He leaned over to hug Pasindu again, then he ambled away. Pasindu opened the box. It was an old, faded pink pencil.

Pasindu watched him leave, his ass muscles tensing through his tight jeans as he strode away. 'Manjula,' he shouted out. 'Did you get the blue one?'

Old Boys' Nuts

When Danuja Liyanage stormed through the high arches of the Monsoon Lodge clubhouse, I turned away and looked over the wall towards the Indian Ocean, where fishing boats bobbed up and down in the glow of the setting sun. I knew this day would come because Danuja clearly believed that by hurting me, he was hurting the part of himself that he despised.

If not for the cut glass lined on the parapet wall between where I stood and the ocean, I may have jumped into the water before Danuja found me. Yet, when Hauke, my new boyfriend, placed his hand on my back, and whispered, 'Don't be afraid of that coward,' I had a feeling of safety and acceptance that was most unusual, but most welcome at the same time.

I first met Danuja at his old school's dinner dance. I grew up in England so had never before experienced such mindlessly drunk loyalty, camaraderie and affection amongst same-sex alumni. I tried to fit in as best I could but found it impossible to keep up with their proficient and over-enthusiastic consumption of alcohol.

Under a disco ball on the dance floor of the Samavanna Hotel ballroom, the former Isthuthi College boys, mostly in long, pointed shoes, stuck their limbs out in unusual directions to the strains of the papare band's rendition of 'She'll Be Coming Round the Mountain'. When the old boys sang along they stopped to giggle at the words, 'When she comes.' Most of them seemed to stare through each other, so Danuja stood out as the one man who could still focus with his bloodshot eyes.

Like most of his batchmates, he had large nostrils which flared every time a beat shifted. His eyes were slightly oriental, suggesting that he wasn't the thoroughbred blue-blooded Sinhalese boy his school prided themselves on. His hair was too styled for a man of his age – waved, layered, spiked all in one and he had a dent in his chin which divided opinion. Personally, I kind of liked it.

Where he was different from his batchmates, who all had rice bellies and double chins, was that he was in excellent shape. He wore a fitted shirt, as men with his kind of biceps tend to do, and he had done up few enough buttons to display the jagged definition between his pectoral muscles.

I wouldn't have been able to guess his age from the unnatural blackness of his hair, but he looked twenty years younger than his pals. They looked sixty, he looked forty, but seeing as they were meant to be the same age, I guessed them all to be fifty.

Danuja must have noticed the drunkest men mobbing me on the dance floor; the odd brush of my arse, or pinch of my cheeks. To be fair it was nothing they weren't also doing to each other. Before I had a chance to dash for the exit, Danuja grabbed my hand and pulled me away.

'This isn't a safe place to be as fair-skinned as you are.' Danuja winked and passed me his glass, which was wet and sticky on the outside. Without thinking about it, I gulped down something I had never had before. It was quite sweet, tasted of coconut and was bloody strong.

'You're not from here, are you?' Danuja asked.

'How can you tell?'

He mimicked the face I'd just made. 'You've never had arrack before.'

I smiled and tucked my chin into my chest. Danuja's gaze constantly shifted between me and a lady at a table on the far side of the room. She sat alone, like a jilted bride, in a white sari with turquoise floral print and gold hems. Her skin looked like white coffee, milkier than mine, and her hair was pulled back in a compact bun. She looked towards us and stood up, lifting her sari far enough to one side to display her bloody amazing abs. I guess she thought she could intimidate me.

Well, she could. I don't work out for nothing, and am rather proud of my abs, but it was her breasts that

I envied. They bulged out of her sari jacket, perky and firm enough to park a bike between. She lifted up even more of her sari, showing off high heels I had no interest in until she tripped over them as she stumbled out of the ballroom.

Danuja clapped his hands together. 'She hates these things. Real killjoy. Anyway, now she's left to pick up our son –' he twirled me around '– so the fun begins.'

'Okay,' I said. I felt dizzy from either the arrack or the dancing. 'But since you're married, you're just getting one dance from me.'

I drank enough arrack that night to forget that Danuja was married. I drank even more and woke up in bed with him on the seventh floor of the Samavanna Hotel. He left before I had finished pulling up my underpants and, a man who claimed to be in hospitality and had a head like a Malteser, put me in a cab with a couple of Russian ladies.

Even though I hadn't given Danuja my number, I was convinced that he'd find me. In Colombo, everyone knows everyone and no one can hide. Yet he didn't come looking. I waited two weeks before I gave up on him, then a further two weeks before I gave up on giving up on him.

I was still staying with my cousin, whose husband's brother's gym buddy, Cuckoo Siva, was an old boy of Isthuthi College, so I could have tracked down Danuja if

I wanted to. I wanted to, believe me, but I was too proud to go knocking on bedroom doors asking for encores.

I didn't fancy bumping into Danuja when he was with his wife, so I became a recluse, skipping all of Colombo's most popular social events such as fashion shows and funerals. Yet, I couldn't keep holding my cousin off and eventually I agreed to go with her crew (she was a flight attendant) to Jazz Sunday at the Colombo Cricket Club grounds.

Walking down the steps of the pavilion and onto the outfield, I accepted a plastic glass of vodka cranberry from Cuckoo Siva. He lectured me about Sri Lanka's precious sapphires as if I would be interested. I tried my best to nod along but, against my better judgment, I couldn't help looking for Danuja. Right then, as the next band tuned their instruments, a hush descended over the ground. People started tapping each other on the shoulder, pointing in the direction of Danuja's wife. Bitch Queen, as I liked to call her, rested against the hoardings that demarcated the pitch's boundary. An advertisement poster of her sipping an Elephant House Ginger Beer towered above where she stood sipping an Elephant House Ginger Beer.

Okay, I thought, *I get it, you're a bloody model*, but like my un-PC cousin told me, 'Being a model in this town is like having the biggest eyes in China. It doesn't mean much.'

Bitch Queen turned and leaned her butt cheeks on the hoardings. Her white dress was cut from just above her bum to her shoulders and the feminine muscularity of her back fought for attention against the honey colour of her skin. She did a Marilyn Monroe wave to someone near us and everyone at Jazz Sunday, apart from me, waved back. Or so it seemed. A dark man with fuzzy long hair guided her through a gap in the boundary boards, onto the pitch and towards a table.

To my left, a group of women shared my laughter when Bitch Queen's ridiculously high heels got stuck in the turf. The man with her had to bend down to pull her shoe out of the mud, requiring such force that he ended up elbowing her in the knee. This caused her to bend down in pain, flashing the top of her bum crack through that oh-so-sexy gap on the back of her dress.

As I sipped my drink, I saw Danuja through the bottom of my plastic glass. He leaned forward to kiss his wife, but I don't think their lips touched.

I picked up a jug of vodka cranberry and poured myself another drink which I downed faster than the first. Before I knew it, I was swaying like a palm tree in the breeze to the twines of a drugged-out bass guitarist. That's when Danuja looked at me. I lifted my hand to wave at him but then withdrew it, pretending the gesture to be part of my dance. He looked towards his wife but she had turned to show off her back to anyone who hadn't yet seen it. Danuja grinned like a naughty schoolboy and gave her a pat on the backside, which looked suspiciously like a slap. He then picked up a crate of Lion Lager and a cricket bat and whistled to a group of friends to join him on the middle of the pitch.

Three drinks later I sat, alone, under the forty-foot-high scoreboard with my drink perched on a precarious plastic table that was missing a leg. Danuja batted on the other side of the outfield from me, giving catching practice to a group of teenagers who looked more unsteady on their feet than perhaps they should have done at their age.

Resting the blade of his cricket bat above his brow, Danuja looked in my direction. He lobbed a tennis ball in the air and took a huge swing at it. The ball sailed towards my table, forcing me to shield my face with my arms. He marched towards the scoreboard, the bat on his shoulder, and pulled up a chair next to me.

'I have to make this quick, because my wife has eyes on both her faces.' Danuja leaned in to hug me, smacking me on the back as if I was one of his old school friends.

'I don't want to wreck anyone's marriage,' I said.

'She doesn't even like me.' He looked around, left and right. 'Just likes the idea of us being in magazines together.'

I lifted up my glass to hide my smile.

Danuja slapped my leg under the table as if to test the waters. 'Was Cuckoo Siva hitting on you?'

'I'm not his type,' I said.

'That punk fancies anything that moves.'

'Thanks for the compliment.'

'You know what I mean.' He gripped my wrist harder than I would have expected. 'Stay away from him, okay?'

'Or what?'

Danuja took a deep breath and laughed. 'I thought you must have gone back to England.'

'Are you happy I didn't?'

'It depends.' He moved opposite me and rubbed my bare legs with his hairy toes. 'Do you want to meet again?'

'I'm not that easy.'

'Come on, you have to admit you had fun.' He gave me that knock-out, mischievous smile of his. The kind of smile you assume is fake, but it's so damn good you want to believe it's real.

'I don't remember much,' I said.

'You want me to remind you?'

I bit the inside of my cheeks. 'Dream on, brother.'

Forty-seven minutes later I was naked on his bed in an apartment his wife thought he kept to rent out on Airbnb.

My cousin has never been the sharpest thorn on the pineapple, but even she worked out that I was seeing someone. Part of me worried that, having seen me with him at Jazz Sunday, she may have suspected Danuja, but it transpired that she, like everyone else, thought he had the happiest marriage in postcolonial Sri Lanka.

At the beginning I worried that he might have been sleeping around with others, but after two months of strenuous love-making I doubted he could have the energy. Besides, he displayed such jealousy whenever I so much as spoke to another man, I was confident he was in love with me. Whenever I told him that I could not go on hiding like this he promised me the world but demanded patience. Yet, I had to have more than just the sex, because as much as I loved him, I needed romance. I dreamt of having at least one meal with him in public to put some kind of rubber stamp on our relationship.

Initially he refused this request but then I stopped turning up at his flat. This led to him sending me lovey-dovey text messages, which morphed into drunken abuse. It was jarring getting a message that said, 'I know you're sleeping with other men, you slut,' but I made excuses for him. I knew how hard it would be for him to come out and say he was with me and that he was leaving his wife and child. I knew how he was drinking to deal with this. Yet, I should have heard the warning bells when he called me to say he would beat the crap out of me unless I came to his flat right at that very moment.

The next morning, as always, he was apologetic in the extreme but I wanted to ignore him and could have done so until he agreed to meet me for a very early lunch at the Cricket Cafe. We sat on stools either side of a beer barrel that served as our table. As soon as Danuja lit his fourth cigarette without a break, I knew this meeting was a mistake. He couldn't bring himself to look me in the eye, and the only time he touched me was when he cupped his hands around mine as I lit matches for him.

Throughout our time there his eyes darted back and forth, left and right. The occasional foreigner arrived for a solo beer, but that wasn't the kind of person he was hiding from. So he breathed out a little and leaned back, only to jump to his feet again when his son's French teacher sauntered into the main bar. She caught his eye and waved before he had a chance to turn his back on her. Instead, he stumbled over to her table and was quick to explain who I was. 'Work colleague,' he said. 'You here to watch French cricket?'

She followed his laughter even though I doubt she understood the joke. Even if she did it was unworthy of any more than a slight grin.

'Join us,' Danuja said to her, which was plain rude and disrespectful to me.

'No, thanks, I'll be fine over here.' She tried to look down at her menu, but clearly sensed Danuja's eyes on her. 'I'm just waiting for the other teachers. They're still at Barefoot Gallery for –'

'Oh bugger.' Danuja slapped the back of his hand against his head. 'For inter-house art. I'm meant to be there.'

'Your son won his category.'

'Excuse me.' Danuja pulled out his phone as he exited the bar.

Seconds later he strode back in, panting and looking over his shoulder. He didn't re-join my table, and instead sat down with his son's French teacher. He leaned forward and held her wrist and said, 'He's on his way here.'

It became obvious that Danuja would rather his son caught him snuggled up to this hot French girl than with me. Two could play at that game. I moved over to the bar counter, where a good-looking Aussie sat alone watching the cricket. I made sure Danuja could see me smacking the Australian on the back as I laughed at his jokes. I noticed Danuja watching, but he left soon after and so did I.

I strolled towards a parked tuktuk, but I couldn't find the driver. I was about to turn away, but Danuja appeared from behind a tree and pushed me into the back seat with his sweaty fingers digging into my neck. He pulled down the flaps on either side of the tuktuk so no one could see in, then pulled my hair and kissed me.

I managed to slap his hand off. 'Leave me alone.'

'Why?' he asked. 'Because I'm not white?'

He lunged for me again, and I let him kiss me a little but when the tuktuk driver returned and lifted the flaps, I took the chance to get out and run off.

I avoided his calls for four days, but he tracked me down and invited me to spend a weekend at a friend's beach bungalow near Galle. I knew I had to say no. I knew I had to get out of this toxic situation; say goodbye to him for good.

But we don't always do what we know to be right.

Danuja got to the bungalow before me so that he could send the staff off. He told me to come after dark which, as it turned out, I did three times. After that we sat wrapped in one sheet on the empty beach, watching the reflection of the full moon wobble on the ocean.

'You will never tell anyone about what we have, no?'

I laughed and nibbled at his ear. 'I just might if you don't leave your wife.'

'It's not that easy,' he said.

'Well, eventually I will have to move on if you don't.'

'Don't say that.' Danuja stroked my hand. 'There is no one else, is there?'

'I have suitors, yes.'

'But –'

'But I don't look at them like I do you.'

Danuja closed his eyes and took in deep breaths. I could see a vein popping on the side of his neck, while he ground his teeth. 'Do you spend time with other men?'

'I have friends.'

'Platonic?' he asked.

'At least for now.'

'What does that mean?' Danuja stood up and leaned over me, blocking out the moon's beam. 'What the hell does that mean?'

'Just sit down, man,' I said. 'You're scaring me.'

'Have you been hanging out with Cuckoo Siva?'

I didn't say anything as there didn't seem to be any good answer.

He grabbed my hair and pulled me to my feet. 'I said, have you been hanging around with Cuckoo Siva?' Pushing at my shoulders, he let go of my hair.

'He's very close to my cousin's family.'

'Have you slept with him?'

'What the hell's wrong with you?'

He grabbed my throat. 'Have you bloody slept with him?'

I couldn't breathe because his hand was squeezing the air out of me. But, I also kind of gave up and accepted the pain. I couldn't be bothered to argue. I felt like everything was over. There was no point in me being at this beach bungalow; there was no point in my being in Sri Lanka if all I ever had to do was hide.

When he let go of my neck, he still looked like he wanted to beat the crap out of me so I turned on my heels and staggered up the beach to the bungalow.

'Did he try to kiss you?' he called out.

I had had enough. 'Yes, he couldn't keep his hands off me. He touched me all over. He ripped off my clothes and lay me down –'

And then without me noticing, Danuja grabbed my balls and was breathing down my neck from behind. 'Did he touch these?'

I was on my face, eating sand as he pressed my head down. His hands pulled at the elastic of my shorts. I couldn't beat him off. As hard as I tried. Two men, of equal size, but something in his head made him so much more powerful than me.

I gave him more chances, I don't know why. I had no one to talk to about him. I hadn't come out to my family, so how could I bring this up with anyone? He was the only person in Sri Lanka who knew my secret. Maybe I was one of the few that knew his. I guess I didn't need to speak to anyone as all they would tell me is what I already knew. I had to leave him. Not answer his calls. Not write him letters. Not apologize for things I hadn't done.

I got a job at a school and every day when I finished teaching he would be there to watch me go home. Sometimes I would speak to him, sometimes I wouldn't, but I always wanted him there. The one time he didn't come I worried that he didn't love me anymore so I called him and the next thing I knew he was drunk and calling me a slut.

At first, whenever he beat me, I thought he could not control himself. In fact, I almost felt sorry for him and took all the blame. I knew he hated himself for being with me, because I reminded him of who he really was and that destroyed him. Yet, when I realized he was calculated enough never to hit me again in the face, or anywhere else it would show, it was clear he knew what he was doing. By hitting me, he was hitting himself. By hitting me where the pain would linger longest he was hitting the parts of himself he was ashamed of and maybe that's why he often went for my balls.

But I still kept seeing him, because when he was calm, he showed me more love than I had ever seen before. At my weakest, I liked him being obsessed with me as it was better than when men just used me and moved on. I had been cheated on in every relationship I ever had, with men and women, and I knew he would never do that to me. He would be loyal. I knew he hated his wife and, for once, I had no competition for a lover's affection.

And things got better. He didn't hurt me for a few weeks and I really believed he had come to terms with his own sexuality and this made him calmer.

Then one evening I arrived at his flat before him and got straight in the shower. I locked the door, without really knowing that I did, which in the end saved me from what could have been my greatest-ever beating.

He tried to kick the door open. 'You bloody gay bastard.' He slurred his words. 'You disgust me and God will punish you.'

'And you?' He couldn't see me but I still scrunched up my nose and put my hands out to the side, palms up like a Kandyan dancer.

'You're all the bloody same.' He tried to say 'promiscuous' but was too drunk. 'You think you're the queen of the town. I know you. I know you. And I will kill you.'

I kept the shower on and slumped into the corner of the cubicle, as he threw everything he had at the door. I waited till he left, but did not come out of the bathroom for another hour just in case. At that moment I knew I could never see him again.

When school holidays came around, I checked into one of the guest rooms at Monsoon Lodge. They had a foreigners-only policy so Danuja was not allowed past reception, but I was because of my British passport.

Monsoon Lodge became my sanctuary. I frazzled away in the sun with my white friends, losing the fairness of my skin that others in the country would have cherished. The expats there tended to be in the country on two- or three-year contracts so they didn't have time to judge me, or to subscribe to the kind of prejudice that eats away at our society. It was good to talk about things I loved, and to be able to play with children without worrying that I could never have my own. It was good not to have to worry about what aunty this or uncle that thought of my lifestyle choices.

While I had Monsoon Lodge, I could still be happy, but Danuja managed to take that away from me. For a two-week period, every time I left the club in a tuktuk, I saw his MG just outside the car park. Jinesena, the smiley security guard, told me that the man behind the wheel drove past the club all through the night. Every night. I found this to be terrifying and I began to understand that it wasn't jealousy. I genuinely believed that Danuja wanted to kill me because then he could kill the part of himself he detested. Everything about our relationship was secret. He would have preferred people to know he punched rather than kissed me. Far more macho. Far more socially acceptable.

I hated myself for what I had done to him; I hated myself for what I had become – a man too weak to come out even though one of my eighteen-year-old students had. Even though all my students as good as knew I was gay.

When I was sixteen, my parents were ashamed of who they thought I had become, so they sent me to England. I waited to return to Sri Lanka until I no longer needed to hide from myself, but that was all Danuja made me do.

With help from Hauke, I refused to hide anymore.

That night Danuja entered Monsoon Lodge, his arrogance was matched only by his fear of embarrassment, but I knew one day he would flout the admittedly reprehensible foreigners-only policy.

'No more hiding,' Hauke said into my ear. He looked around the lodge grounds and did the one thing Danuja never had the balls to do. He held my face, stroked my beard and kissed me, bang on the lips, in front of everyone.

Loyal Stalker

HER LEGS ARE defined, her arms skinny, her breasts like bang-bang-come-in. I want to wrap her chocolate brown hair around my neck, bite it at the ends. I want to put my forehead against hers, look into her slanted eyes; kiss the end of her sharp nose.

I close my eyes and smell the air around her. Unusual for someone so wealthy, she does not wear perfume made in the name of a big-assed celebrity. Instead she smells of citronella mosquito repellent.

She's taller than me by three inches so must be about five-foot-five. And if I'm as black as a tropical islander can get, she's as fair. I love pale skin because I can see the veins during a workout. I can't wait to see her lift weights; can't wait for her veins to bulge.

She's with Loku Master, our gym manager, my boss. He has just done a workout in his shirt and tie, so he smells like a bag of sweat. 'Take your pick,' he says.

I'm lined up with the other personal trainers. There's Bicep Badula, Deadlift Dilshan, Ab-crunch Asoka and me, Chin-up Channa. Together, we're the Hard Body Crew by day and the Disco Dons by night.

She paces up and down looking at us, as if we are pairs of shoes in a fancy-ass shop. She stops at me and bends to look at my legs. I am shorter than the others, and my chest isn't as full but when it comes to quads and calves, I am one of the best in Sri Lanka.

'Can I have this one, please?' she says with her head bowed, looking up seductively.

'This is Chin-up Channa,' Loku Master says.

'Pleasure to meet you, Channa. I am Dilini.' She holds her hand out to me and I grab it in a limp grip. *Grip hard, punk*, I tell myself too late.

Loku Master says, 'You want someone who won't try to chat you up –'

'I didn't mean –'

'Channa's the man. Two years he's worked for me. Never heard him utter a word to a lady.'

She looks at me like I'm a lost puppy stuck in a drain.

'No, he can speak,' Loku Master says. 'Just very shy. Very respectful. He'll instruct you with claps and nods.'

What he says about my respect for women is true and I want to show her that but I also want to bite her ass. Instead I lead her into the gym. She looks concerned that, with so many large windows, anyone from the street can see in. 'The cardio section's a bit hot,' I say, 'because the cool from the air-conditioners travels downstairs. Fault in design.'

'Sorry, did you say something?'

I giggle. I think she's flirting with me already.

I get on the cross trainer and use the touchscreen to enter her details. It asks for her age. 'Twenty-four,' she says and I type it in.

Weight? 'Forty-eight kilos.'

I programme in the time. Thirty minutes, but then I think I'll miss her so I make it twenty. Even that's too long.

'Only four minutes' cardio?' she asks.

I clap my hands and press the start button and she's off.

I walk backwards, lean against the bikes and watch her muscles work; the separation between her butt cheeks; the lines of her thighs. I want to get onto my knees, by the side of the machine, and let her sweat drip on the back of my neck. *Snap out of it, Chin-up Channa*, I tell myself. *You're a professional, not a pervert.*

Time up, so I start walking towards the weights section.

'Should I follow you?' she asks.

'Always,' I say but she doesn't hear.

'Follow, madam,' Bicep Badula says, a smile under his boxer's nose. 'Chin-up Channa doesn't speak to ladies.'

I set up the Smith Machine for her to do squats. I show her one, my ass touching the back of my shoes as I lower myself down.

'All the way?' she asks.

I smile. 'Oh yeah, baby.' I clap which is her cue to start and I hold her hips as she goes up and down.

My eyes closed, I breathe her in and with each rep she does, with each grunt and groan, with each bead of sweat, I love her more. She is taking this workout seriously, and that means she respects me. Respect's what I am about.

This is the beginning of the perfect relationship.

She told me she'd come every day. I saved a slot for her; cancelled my cash-cow booking; shaved my beard, my legs, my toes and chest for her. Bought imported talcum powder, waxed my hair in spikes for her. Showered twice for her. Printed out workouts and diet plans for her. Laminated them for her.

And she stands me up? *Come on, baby girl. This shit ain't right. We've come too far to be playing games here, no? Do you want to have the perfect body or not?*

I drag Deadlift Dilshan outside. 'Get me her number.'

'Take your hands off my shirt,' he says. 'Calm down, okay? Take a breath.'

I face the wall, pound it with my fists. 'Get me the damn number.'

'Whose number?' he asks.

'Dilini's.'

'The new member whose ass you –'

' – the number, please, bro.'

'Don't have it,' he says.

'Get it from the bloody computer, champ.'

'Your voice is even more high-pitched than normal, machang. Take a bloody breath.'

'Please,' I say. 'I'll distract Loku Master. You go in, get her number.'

Deadlift Dilshan laughs. 'Hell, bro, why don't I distract him, you go in?'

'Champ, please, you owe me,' I say. Punk does owe me. Bugger had no veins left to inject his steroids into yesterday so I had to find him one on his penis. I point to it. 'Even things out.'

He gets me her number and I make the call and she says, 'Hello, hello, hello, is anyone there?' but she doesn't hear me so I put that phone away and pull out my work mobile and type out this message: 'Madam, you missed your class. You come tomorrow?'

But she doesn't reply. I wait ten more seconds. Still no reply. Another ten. As they say a watched phone never beeps so I close my eyes. Count to twenty. Nothing. *What is this, baby? If you are to trust me with your body, you have to play by my rules.*

Ping. My phone. 'Sorry Channa, I'm exhausted. Barely slept. I'll come tomorrow at eight?'

It's eight in the morning and she's nowhere to be seen. Does she know I've been up waiting since six?

She's not taking this seriously. Not taking the gym seriously. Not taking us seriously. I lift up a barbell and curl so much weight my biceps scream and then ...

Oh my God. I smell the citronella. My legs buckle below me and I haven't even done squats yet. I try not to smile too much, but it's easier said than done.

To be honest, I wish she had not exposed so much skin. It's not just me here; there are other men who are going to try to look at her cleavage and I haven't got eyes on my lats. It's a nice sports bra, sure, and I like the camouflage print, but she should have worn a t-shirt on top.

'I've been dreading this,' she says. 'Had a very bad night's sleep again, but I know that's not going to stop you pushing me to my limits.'

I clap my hands and walk upstairs to the cardio section and she follows. I give her five minutes this time, and I sit on the bike behind her, happy to be watching until she picks up her phone to answer a call.

'Hello, Ammi,' she says. 'It doesn't matter if she doesn't finish her milk.'

I get off the bike and stand by her side, clapping to make her go faster. She looks down at me, shakes her head at me, like she's pissed off I'm disturbing her, but *hello, this isn't a day at the spa, princess.*

She holds her hand to the phone. 'This is important. It's about my baby.'

Your what, what, what? No. No. No. She can't be married. She can't be, because if she is why did she flirt with me? Why did she wear fewer clothes for me? *Tell me it ain't so, baby girl. Or have I read the signs all wrong?*

She ends her call. 'How many more minutes?'

I point to the screen.

'My mother's so annoying. She can't handle waste so calls me if Maria doesn't finish every drop of formula.'

I act out cradling a baby, point at her.

'Yes, I have a baby.' The cross trainer beeps to tell her she's done, so she wipes her face with a towel and gets off the machine. 'Nine months old.'

Life as I know it has ended. How could this be? I cannot share her with another, even in my dreams.

I adjust the seat on the shoulder press, and put it on a weight I know she'll struggle with. I don't like being deceived like this. Each machine we move to I push her harder, but she takes it, without complaint, because she feels guilty. Because she knows she has wronged me.

But the problem is, each time she overcomes a challenge I set her, it just makes me love her more. When she does a forty-pound bench press, I can see the veins between her breasts, bright green. I want to fall on top of her. I want to love her and, if need be, I can wait until she realizes her husband is not Mr Right. What should I do? Maybe these are questions only God, and my prophet, can answer.

Dilini's on her back on a mat, and I push her leg away from me, towards her face. My hands are on her smooth skinned calves. I want to lick the sweat off them. I want to put my teeth around them.

Then she's on her front and I bend her legs forward, to stretch the quads, and I lean over her, watching her backside, until she tells me that I have held her legs in that position for too long. I stand, pulling her arms behind her, so she arches and I can see her face in the mirror, eyes closed, grimacing as if we are making a brother or sister for Maria.

After Dilini leaves, I have a session with Madu. He's a good-looking kid, two years older than me and a foot taller. He acts like he's all refined and well-spoken but his father is a village boy just like me, although he went on to become a smuggler and then one of the most powerful men in the country. You have to like this kid, Madu, because even though he is Cuckoo Siva's son he still talks to everyone. He's been in the papers a fair bit, as he used to be a non-conformist, but not in the mould of other VIP's sons. He's a lover, not a fighter; a smoker, not a drinker, and one day he will inherit his father's empire because he has no brothers and his mother's a slut. Much to his father's publicized annoyance, at twenty-two he is still out and about with different women every night, but he wants to settle down, he tells me. The only problem is he can't find a girl both he and his mother think is attractive enough for him.

Madu is richer than everyone else in the gym combined but he wears out-of-shape t-shirts with stretched necks. These are the kind of t-shirts tourists wear: tributes to Sri Lanka; sketches of men in sarongs carrying coconuts; monkeys swinging from trees; elephants trumpeting.

But Madu is no low-budget tourist. His father owns construction companies, TV stations, newspapers, jewellery shops, helicopters. The only thing he doesn't bloody own is this gym. So yeah, they say he's a catch and a half. Some say he's the most eligible bachelor in Colombo. Others say his arms are short and his pockets are deep. How could he possibly share his wealth with a woman and kids? Just how cheap is Madu? Once he went through a toll booth backwards so that the person in the passenger seat had to pay.

After the workout, Madu calls me to the shower room to stretch him. He is naked but for an extremely small towel.

'That girl you were training this morning,' he says. 'Dilini, no?'

I stand in front of him, my fists clenched. I am worried because Madu is the only cat in the gym who doesn't purr when Dilini walks by. He's ice-cool with her. 'How do you know who she is?'

'Her ex-husband is on my pub quiz team.'

I smile. 'She's not married anymore?'

'Technically, maybe.' Madu lifts his foot onto the bench to stretch his quads. 'But only because divorce takes a while. Her husband's a good bugger, but he cheated on her while she was pregnant. They married when she was nineteen.'

I say, 'Cheated on –'

'Asked him why,' Madu says.

'And?'

'He said he didn't want to.' Madu puts his towel between his legs and motions for me to pull from either side. 'That he knew it wasn't right to be cheating on a lady carrying his child.'

'Then why'd the bastard bitch do it?

'Because his mistress complained. Said it wasn't her damn fault he knocked up his wife.'

I feel a sense of relief. My dream girl is available. I don't normally go for leftovers, but shit bro, Dilini is an exception in every *single* way. I contemplate what I will do to her shit-for-brains coward husband, but that can wait. I have a love story to star in first.

She cancels her workout again, but this time she texts me to explain.

'Maria woke up seven times,' she writes.

'For milk?' I ask.

'Yes, and also because she keeps turning herself over and getting into positions she can't get out of.'

'Is okay, madam,' I text. 'When she sleeps through nite then u cum everyday.'

'Lol, sure.'

Because I have a free slot, Madu asks me to kill his legs. He is in shorts and this is the first time he has exposed his burnt-matchstick legs in public. Sri Lankans have skinny legs. In fact, we store all our fat around our bellies and none on our limbs. Ab-crunch Asoka thinks this is because it's a hot country; in cold countries those chunky white dudes have fat spread round to keep them warm. That makes sense to me. Maybe that's why rich, fair chicks like Dilini have fuller legs. Maybe she has some white blood in her from when the Portuguese, the Dutch or the English ruled us.

'I'll do anything you tell me to,' Madu says, 'but no bloody squats.'

I point at his legs. 'Then people will never stop laughing at those twigs.'

'People laugh at me?'

'Do you want big legs?' I ask.

'I want big legs,' he says. 'Please.'

'Then call a driver.'

Turning to the other instructors, Madu asks, 'This bugger for real? Why do I need a driver?'

'To drive your car home,' I say, 'because if you work your legs properly you won't be able to walk, let alone drive. The accelerator will feel like a two-tonne rock to you.'

'Let's hit it,' he says.

After four sets of squats he holds his mouth and looks like he will vomit. I direct him to the leg-press machine but he tries to buy a longer break by talking. 'Met Dilini at a club last night.'

'Dilini?' I ask.

'Yes, Dilini.'

'Dilini de Saram?'

'Yes, you jackass, your client.' Pulling out his wallet, Madu shows me an ID card. 'Hers. She left it on my table at the club. Must be a sign.'

I want to poke Madu's eyes out. 'A sign of what?'

'Well, you know, if she left it on purpose maybe she's saying she, you know ...'

'What, boss, what?'

'That she likes me.'

It is my turn to hold my hand to my mouth. 'But she knew she had a session with me today and she has a goddamn baby. Why the hell was she at a nightclub last night?'

'Everyone's life doesn't revolve around the gym.'

'Pull the other one,' I say. I excuse myself and go round the corner to call her.

'Why are you trying to hurt me?' I ask. *'More importantly, why are you trying to hurt yourself?'*

'Hello, hello,' she says.

'If you're trying to test me you don't need to,' I say. *'If you're trying to make me want you more –'*

'Hello,' she says. 'Listen you prick, it's not nice to call up girls and just breathe heavily into the phone. You call again and I'll tell the police.'

I put this phone away, pull out my work mobile and text her, 'You cum tomorrow, 8?'

'Yes, for sure, assuming Maria sleeps,' she replies. 'I really want to get stronger.'

She's late again but, you know what, that's the least of my worries. As a woman, she really shouldn't be going to nightclubs. It disgusts me, to be damn straight. I feel like giving her a piece of my mind. But then I see her and, like a 700-hundred-pound squat, she takes my breath away. She's glowing, maybe having been in the sun, so her milk-tea-coloured skin is less creamy. She's wearing grey contact lenses and has tinted her hair so it is streaked with auburn.

I'm touched. I'm touched that she has dressed up for me, done her hair and her eyes for me. I've made an effort too. *See these shoes?* Brand spanking new, just for her. My teeth whitened for her, my pits shaved for her, my chest waxed for her.

I'm Chin-up Channa and I'm a badass professional. There is a time and a place to tell her how to dress and how to behave, but for the here and now, my job is to sculpt a body. I give her a laminated traps-lats-and-delts personalized schedule.

'So delts are?' she asks.

'Deltoids,' I say.

'Sorry?'

I touch her shoulders. Then when she says, 'Traps?' I put my hands either side of her neck and when she says, 'Lats?' I start my hands under her arms and want to massage down to her waist but she jumps out of my reach.

'Got it,' she says. 'I'm in good hands. Help me look great, okay?'

That's why I'm here, baby girl, to show you how to do things, to guide you, to mould you physically and mentally; the perfect body, the perfect wife, the perfect mother. I'm so excited.

I start her off with bent-over-lat-raises to work her rear delts. She's a natural and her muscles are tell-your-god-about-great. The ripples, the separation, the tension, the goddamn chemistry.

I move around in front of her, clapping once for each rep, and I see her face, her grimace, the beads of sweat, the effort, the desire, the hunger. She's too good to be true, and of all the damn beautiful bodies on our staff, she chose me.

I show her to the lat pull-down and stand over her while she squeezes out rep after rep after bloody rep and she moans, like a symphony, like a dolphin, like a hamper of gorgeous sounds and I close my eyes and nod with the rhythm, breathing her in, inhaling her.

I open my eyes and follow a drop of sweat down her neck, her upper pecs, into her sports bra, between her cleavage and I can see down the gap between her breasts.

She pulls at loose skin around her abdomen. 'Whatever I eat, however I diet, however I work out,' she says, 'I can't get rid of this.'

'I already have plans,' I say, but she doesn't hear me.

'It's from having a baby, you know,' she says. 'Breastfeeding helped me shed calories, but this skin and these stretch marks won't go.'

She's opening up to me. Sharing her insecurities. Maybe I can trust her with mine. My squeaky voice, my shaky English, my lack of protection as a child.

She crosses her hands either side of her chest and holds at a tiny bit of fat squeezing out of the back of her sports bra. 'And how the hell do I get rid of these? Lat pull-downs?'

'No. To lose fat, we can't target those areas. We just have to kill fat with cardio.'

She places her hands either side of my shoulders, so I tense my delts. 'Wait, Channa, wait. I heard a few words you said there. You said fat?'

I nod and she smiles.

'You said cardio?'

I tense my muscles.

'Oh my bloody God, have I got you talking?' She hugs me so tight I almost fart. 'Am I the first girl you've ever spoken to?'

I go to church to do a job on a non-believer for my master, Prophet Conrad Cecil. I ask him about Madu and he tells me he's a punk like his father and I should not trust Dilini with him.

So I inject roids into Bicep Badula's ass crack and he owes me enough to steal her address from the system.

And here I am in the dead of night, and hell, she lives so close to the gym she makes my life easy. I have stocked myself up with a flask of protein powder and a boiled whole chicken. The empty land opposite her house is so handy and I'm pleased for all the wild bushes to hide behind. I plop down a yoga mat, flattening out the grass and weeds and I light a mosquito coil.

As the moon flashes brighter, I explore. There is a spot on the bare land from where I can see over her gate and then through the grills above her sitting room windows and into the upstairs landing. There is a giant

TV stretched across the wall and Dilini walks up and down, watching what's on, cradling a baby in her arms.

She hands the baby to a lady with a bob haircut and a pair of glasses. Maybe a nanny? Or her mother? Dilini ambles past the TV into a room and the lights go off. Two hours later, the baby cries and the lights come back on, and then the crying stops and I wonder whether Dilini has put her breast to the baby's mouth. Soon the lights are back off again, and I lie back on my mat, look up to the stars, and smile. *I love our life together.*

The Hard Body Crew meet at Independence Square with a few stragglers from the Ripped Gang. After we have done with a round of chest bumps and high fives, we convene a meeting around a lion carved out of stone.

The topic? Our pilgrimage to Thailand.

The reason? To become real men.

Bicep Badula has been before and he tells us that he was very popular there. He'd work out at a gym owned by a former Mr Universe by day, and at night he would strut the street, giving it the walk, giving it the pump, and women wearing very little would lean out of bars calling for him to come in.'

'In Thailand they even have women who are also men,' he says. 'They call it multi-tasking.'

My friends lean forward, fascinated, like Badula is introducing them to another world.

'Channa,' Deadlift Dilshan says, 'why so quiet?'

'I'm listening,' I say.

'You need this more than anyone,' Badula says. 'You have not even kissed a girl.'

'Shut up, champ, of course I have.'

'First show me you can talk to a bird, then maybe I'll believe you can kiss.'

'I'm just not in any rush.'

'In Thailand,' Bicep Badula says, 'the women don't waste time. When I was there I sexed seven different women in four nights.'

'No way,' Dilshan says.

'I swear on my Mr Sri Lanka thong.'

'Girls there like brown skin?'

'They love it, bro. I could have sexed more even but the thing is it's expensive.'

'I don't think I'll come,' I say.

'You have got to be kidding me.' Dulith cups my balls. 'Are you a gay?'

'He's in love,' Badula says. 'Bloody idiot thinks that hot rich bitch –'

I lunge at Badula, push him down onto the ground and shove stones in his mouth until he spits them out. 'Don't call her a bitch.'

'Okay, okay. Get off me.'

I roll off him, hugging my legs, my head between them.

Dilshan strokes my back. 'Dude, whatever we do, however much we earn, to people like Dilini we're just village boys.'

'She's different,' I say. 'She loves me for who I am.'

The Hard Body Crew and all the members of the Ripped Gang stop what they're doing and stare at me. Then each of them looks left and right, then back at me and I can see their eyes smile before they burst out in violent, high-pitched laughter.

Prophet Conrad Cecil tells me that there are evil forces conspiring against me and the Devil wants to snatch me from God's grasp. He tells me to be vigilant. To protect what I have, and all I have are my muscles and my Dilini.

I am training Madu and when he slips me twenty rupees I see that Dilini's ID card is still in his wallet. Why would he not give it back? Surely she needs it. So I offer to rub down his shoulders and back which requires him to lie face down on the mat. I steal the ID card with ease.

I am back outside Dilini's house but she's not here. I know this because her little Nissan March is not parked on the bare land. I watch a group of wild monkeys climb from one house, using the electricity cables, over to her roof. I pull myself up the electricity post and over the wall into her garden.

Her garage is to the left of me through a steel barred gate and her car's not in there either and for good reason: there is no space. Old fridges on their sides, rusted pans, broken flower pots, empty coffee jars, cereal boxes, old cassettes, broken gym equipment, children's toys, newspapers, sewing machines, bags of clothes. This is like a playground for the rats I can hear partying in the junk.

I look towards the house and even though it appears to have been built to be open and airy, every window is protected by steel bars. I climb back over the wall onto the road and wait six hours, that's how much I love her. I miss two personal trainer sessions – two thousand rupees – but that's okay because what's the point of money if I can't spend it on Dilini?

Her silver Nissan March, which she calls her 70's Ho-mobile (because the licence plate is H01978) skids round the blind corner, overshooting the bare land, but in one smooth motion, she reverses the car back into it, killing the engine.

Fiddling with her handbag to find her house keys, she looks up and sees me standing outside her gate and she squints as if not quite believing her luck.

I open her car door and offer to help her carry the shopping from the passenger seat, but she waves me away.

'What are you doing here, Channa?' She balances her shopping on the roof of the car as she locks her door. 'You're scaring me a bit. Should I be scared?'

I laugh. It's a deep laugh I have been practising. 'It's not a big deal, but I found a gym member with this.' I hand over her ID card.

She drops her shopping behind the gate. 'Oh my God, I've been looking for this everywhere.' She hugs me and I want the world to end right now because it is perfect.

'But who had it?' she asks. 'I thought I left it at a nightclub.'

I pull my fingers across my lips so she knows I cannot tell her. 'Madu,' I say.

She struggles to look me in the eye during our next workout. I can tell she feels guilty about something and I wonder if she has been spending time at nightclubs again.

While on the cross trainer, she chats to Madu as if nothing has happened. I know she cleared it up with him and he lied saying he just forgot to give it to her, but come on, how gullible can you be? *Stop bloody talking to him and focus on your heart rate.*

Her handbag is open on the floor next to the cross trainer and I see her house keys. I know what I am about to do is wrong and a breach of a personal trainer's trust, but she has not been altogether honest with herself either and she needs my protection. I grab the keys and put them in my back pocket.

I lean over her cross trainer and put the time remaining up to thirty minutes. Madu sees this and does the same to his machine, which is a little annoying.

I have no time to analyze that now. Without explaining why, I run down the stairs and jump on Dulith's moped, working it to its maximum speed of 19 kmph till I get to Susil Keycuttera's Co-op Shop and push my way to the front of the queue. The man behind the counter charges one hundred and fifty rupees for a new key. I give him one-sixty so that he works on mine straightaway. He's done in less than a minute.

The keys are back in her bag while she still has eight minutes left on the cross trainer. She doesn't notice me returning and even when I stand right next to her, she only looks at me for a split second, then continues talking to Madu.

'So I'm off to Thailand for the new year,' she says.

'Are you going to invite me?' Madu asks.

'No,' I say, but no one hears.

'Would you come if I did?' Dilini asks.

'I would with more warning, but I'm off to Vegas with my mother.'

'What happens in Vegas stays in Vegas,' Dilini says.

'Oh please,' says Madu. 'What am I going to do with my mother? Who are you going with?'

'No one?' I say.

'Wait,' Madu says. 'I thought you didn't speak in front of women?'

'He does with me.' She ruffles my hair. 'And yes, even though I never told him, I am going alone.'

This is one of those signs Prophet Conrad Cecil has told me to watch out for ever since the day he saved me, as a child, from pure evil.

While Dilini's cooling down, I run to Bicep Badula and tell him that I am on for the gym instructors' trip to Thailand. The gym is closed over Sinhala and Tamil New Year, and if Dilini is not in the country what the hell would I do anyway?

I only hope I can get a visa, which Bicep Badula thinks I can as long as I don't do what Ab-crunch Asoka did last year and note 'jiggy jiggy bang bang' as the purpose for visiting.

Rich people in this country think that if you pay poor people well you are spoiling them. Our basic salaries are fifteen thousand a month. Where we are lucky – and lots of people from where I come from aren't – is that we can charge one thousand rupees per personal training session. We spend a lot on protein shakes, steroids, creatine, and hair gel, but we don't pay rent, electricity, transport, and shit like that. So we can save, and save we have for this trip to Thailand about which I am now very excited.

Our first night there we go to this area called Patpong. We get pulled by lots of women into this dark theatre. It seems Badula is not the only one who is very popular with the ladies here. I think maybe these Thai women like short, dark men with massive muscles. When we go back to our shared hotel room, Badula, Dilshan and Asoka bring one girl each with them but I don't because it's not fair on Dilini.

I wake a few hours later to see my boys arguing with the girls who are now fully dressed. They are asking for money from my gang.

'Why I should pay you?' Badula asks. 'You are acting like hooker women.'

'We are hooker women, man,' one of them says.

'You are hooker women man?' Ab-crunch Asoka asks. 'Like a ladyboy?'

'We give you big discount already, mister.'

'But you never tell us we have to pay. You are not my girlfriend?'

The experience costs us one hundred dollars between the four of us. I try to say that I shouldn't have to contribute, but the others insist I should pay even more because I didn't do any work so I give a little extra.

I check Dilini's Facebook which says she is staying at Ocean Breeze on Lamai Beach in Koh Samui.

There's very little I don't know about her. When we are married I will ask her to be a little more private because at the moment any old pervert can find out where she is. I excuse myself from the boys' trip for a couple of days and take the train and ferry to Samui. A minivan drops me straight in front of the hotel where I am met by a stocky man called Bang Bang, who is the hotel owner. He asks what my budget is and after I tell him he says he'll give me a 'non-AC shit room' in his low-budget hotel next door.

Bang Bang directs me away from his fancy hotel's restaurant because he says they are full even though there is no one there. I thought by leaving Sri Lanka I would no longer be treated so differently. But, you know what, Dilini has given me the confidence to stand up to people. To say, look I'm a human just like you. Don't lock me in a damn dog cage, you know.

'I demand to sit in your fancy restaurant,' I say. 'Nothing you can say will make me move.'

'If you spend three thousand baht, you stay, if not you go.'

'Okay, I'll sit elsewhere, boss.'

Bang Bang sets me up on a plastic table and chair behind a palm tree on the land next door. From here I watch the sea, which is like a swimming pool, so clear I can even see white women's breasts through the water. I zone out, eat some kickass fish and wait for Dilini. I never give up and this pays off for me because soon enough I see her strolling down the beach, a wide-rimmed hat over her face but she's not wearing anything to cover her chest. It is an incredible sight but come on! *What the hell is wrong with you?*

I want to run up and put something over her pecs, but I don't think it is the right time to jump out at her. So I stand up, in line with the tree and she cannot see me. I watch as she passes me and even her backside is visible because her swimsuit is small enough to use to clean between my teeth. *Have I got you wrong, baby girl? How can you show the world your body? I mean, hell I know these guys have small eyes but they can still see.*

She is so close I can smell her sun cream. She walks up the rock stairs to the posh hotel and across a ramp that leads to a wooden bungalow, the front of which appears to be floating over the beach (but it is actually pivoted to a crane hidden behind a tree). I hear the shower come on and I imagine what is happening inside. I must get ready too.

I stand under the bare light bulb in the middle of my room. It reminds me of Coach Uncle's hotel room when he got real angry with me. Dilini is lucky because I'll always be there to hear her screams.

It's the same routine as always. I use my tweezers to pluck the hair between my eyebrows, then I wrap ice in a cloth and put it to my eyes to reduce any puffiness. Now I trim the hair on my knuckles, toes and under my armpits. Then I do some push-ups to get blood pumping into my pecs and arms. I look in the mirror, and boy, I'm good to go.

I walk down to the beach and look towards Dilini's cabin and the door is open. Two smiley Thai maids say something to me and laugh, but it's in another language – probably Thai. I cross the ramp to her door and look into the room. The windows are open so the curtains blow in, and the used sheets and towels flap about on the floor.

But there are no bags. No sign of Dilini.

'Where is the woman who was here before?' I ask the maids.

'Ahahahahahahahahaha,' they say. They don't have a clue what I am talking about.

I run to Reception and catch Bang Bang by the t-shirt. He looks like he may head-butt me in anger. I take my hands off. 'Sorry, sir, I was in a rush.'

He grins, says something in Thai then laughs. Taps me on the back. 'What is up, brother?'

'I'm looking for a girl.'

'Very easy to find girl in Samui. You go to bar with money and you have girl.'

'No, sir, I look for this girl.' I show him a photocopy of Dilini's ID card.

'She is a hot lady. Woo hoo.'

'Yes, very hot,' I say. 'Where is she?'

'She gone, bro. My van drop her at the airport –' he flaps his arms as if they are wings '– and she piss off like a beautiful angel.'

The second I land back in Sri Lanka, I break away from the Hard Body Crew and take a tuktuk to Dilini's house but she's not at home so I use the set of keys I had cut and I open her gate and then struggle with her front door because the locks are rusted and almost off their hinges. Inside, to the left, is her sitting room. There are two sets of metal sofas and two metal armchairs, and a metal and glass table. The metal on all the furniture is white, but slightly rusted. I wonder if I am in the wrong house because I assumed Dilini's family was rich, but all this stuff looks like junk. I guess, from the photos on the wall, that this is her mother's house but why is it like a garbage site?

On the floor is a kid's play mat in the colours of a beach. Around that are three teddies, a box of rattles and a stuffed toy monkey wearing red boots. There are also countless half-blown-up balloons, an electric organ, two standing fans which are, yep, rusted.

To the left, down two stairs is the dining room; by the table are six – yes, six – old cassette players – even us poor people don't use cassette players anymore. Through an arch is the kitchen, the cupboards made of rotting wood painted a sickly blue. There are three fridges; I open each of them – the first is being used as a cupboard for products such as canola oil which expired fourteen years ago. The second one is also off and holds rice bags and onions; the third one is on and is packed with old ice-cream containers and coffee jars of suspect curries.

I go up the stairs; the banisters are white, rusted metal. There is Perspex attached to the metal bars; I guess that is to make sure the baby doesn't fall through the gaps when she crawls. At the top of the stairs, on the left, is a room with a low slanted roof and wooden floors; clothes have been hung to dry in here; there is an ironing board; there are also two cycling machines, a number of weights, medicine balls, cardboard boxes. I'm confused.

To my left is a small room, which is impeccably clean and smells of baby cream. The walls are pink, there are owls painted on the furniture and there is a pristine white cot under a mosquito net.

I enter the room next door. Scent of citronella, the lighting moody, the floor clean. I can smell her.

I lie on her bed; so soft, so silky, so arousing. I take off my shirt, then my track bottoms, then my jungies and I can feel my bare ass against her white cotton sheets.

I walk naked to her cupboard and I lift her dresses to my face and smell. I rub them all over my naked body.

I want to find her panties but then I hear the front gate opening and I am screwed so I grab all my clothes and push a wooden door which opens to a balcony above the sitting room. I jump down and land on the sofa. To my right, up two steps, is another room, which I can barely get into. There is wall-to-ceiling junk, like in the garage. Old lamps, old gym equipment, old washing machines, boxes of clothes, piles of old magazines. It looks like no one comes in here anymore except to stow things away.

This will be my room.

I watch through the louvers. Dilini is in the garden watering plants with baby Maria at her chest in a carrier. Her mother stands in tight gym clothes, pot belly protruding over an inflated baby pool.

'Shall I make biryani for dinner?' Ammi asks.

'I told you a thousand times, I'm trying to be healthy so only fruit and veg for dinner.'

'Ah yes.' Ammi pulls down her t-shirt to cover her rice belly. 'What about mutton curry?'

'Ammi, do you ever listen?'

'You must let yourself go once in a while.'

'You ask me the same thing every single night,' Dilini says. 'Who told you to buy three kilos of meat?'

'It was on special,' she says. 'Because the power had gone so –'

'I'm not going to eat your spoilt meat, Ammi, whatever you say.'

'Okay, how about something western. Mutton burgers?'

'I can't,' Dilini says. 'I can't. If you want me to live in your house you have to listen to me or we'll both go mad.'

I watch Dilini come inside with Maria. She turns on the lights, but then Ammi follows and turns them all off which is good because it makes it easier for me not to be seen.

'Ammi, you're saving ten rupees by turning off that light. You have inherited millions of dollars.'

'How do you know?' Ammi asks, looking up at the roof and water pipes. 'Did you find it?'

'You were telling me to let myself go. What about you?' Dilini climbs the stairs and almost looks back at me so I drop to the floor behind a shoe rack, my head to the ground, thinking, Right, this is it. I've been caught, and I feel relieved that I no longer need to hide. But she doesn't say anything so maybe she didn't see me, or maybe she did and she likes me protecting her.

Dilini goes into her room but storms back out in a matter of seconds. 'What the hell, Ammi, did you go through my clothes again?'

'I was with you, no?'

'Before, while I was swimming.'

'No, I swear.'

'Ammi, seriously, the cupboard's open and my dress is on the floor. I know you want to try on my things so you can say you're fifty and can still fit into my clothes, but it doesn't really impress anyone.'

'I didn't go into –'

'Did you lie on my bed?'

'I swear I didn't.'

'I told you, you need therapy. You need bloody therapy.' She points around the house. 'You need to see someone before your anxieties becomes dangerous.'

The door slams behind Dilini so I go to my new room and use my tricep power to squeeze some boxes against the wall so that I have space to lie down amidst this mess.

I have never slept better.

I don't stay at Dilini's house every night because I need to give her space, I know that. We're still new together and shouldn't move too fast. Besides, I also have to gather evidence to show her that Madu is dating many other women so I follow him from time to time. For example, last night I was invited to man the doors at the opening of Black Cat Cafe and managed to get a selfie which had him in the background holding hands with a blonde lady.

That being said, tonight I am back in her house and when all the lights go off, I have a look around. First I head to the kitchen and try Ammi's biryani which has an odd flavour but it is full of character. Then I pop into the nursery and the baby girl is fast asleep. I put on her night light and see that she has very chubby cheeks, but that's okay at her age. If she is fat when she's older, that's not an issue either. By then she will call me Thathi and I can make her work out and eat well.

The room is a little too cold for her, if I am honest. She may be wrapped up warm, but still. So I turn the air conditioner off. Also, why has Dilini not given the poor girl any pillows? And why is she sleeping on her back? If she brings up any milk she will choke, no?

It's okay. I forgive Dilini. I know she's tired. Before I came on the scene she had to do most of this alone. I turn over little Maria and prop her up against a couple of pillows. Ah. She looks so comfortable now. She's smiling at me. At my orphanage there was this sweet baby and I remember we used to think she was grinning when she was actually doing number two. So I check and yes, she needs a new nappy. I do the needful and then carry her back to sleep.

I close the door quietly behind myself and wander over to Ammi's room. I know she annoys Dilini, but she is like a mother to me too, so I need to see if she is okay. She's on her back, snoring with her mouth wide open. Because her room has no curtains, it is lit up by the street light directly outside. I step on her junk, and something rustles under my foot. Ammi looks directly at me and I smile but I am not sure she can make me out. She rubs her eyes and reaches for her glasses, by which time I am behind the TV-room sofa. Ammi crouches around the house, a torch attached by a strap to her forehead. She is carrying what looks to be a catapult in her hand. After a few minutes of searching she is back snoring in her bed.

Now everyone's asleep and no one is going to disturb us. I enter Dilini's room, and aney, she's so tired she couldn't stay up for me. That's okay. She's still in her day clothes. That's how exhausted she is.

Her bed is massive, and she's curled up into a tiny little ball so I can lie next to her without her even noticing. I run my fingers through her hair, but I am careful not to wake her as she needs the sleep. I let my mouth travel around her body, but it never touches her because I want her to be awake the first time that happens. I try to sleep, but I can't because this moment is so magical.

There's a big noise from the baby monitor by her bed. Maria is crying and I don't want to surprise Dilini so I roll off the bed, and then under it. Dilini turns the light on, and now I can see her beautiful ankles. Her stunning feet. Oh I so want to bite them, but that might shock her.

I'm embarrassed to say this, but I fall asleep under her bed. Really I should have stayed up to help with little Maria. I wake to the sound of the shower and I think about joining Dilini in it but, *hey baby, let's take things slow.* So I watch her through the gap she left open in the bathroom door. *Do you know I'm here? I think you must. I think you want me to watch.*

I have never seen anything more beautiful in my life. The soap running down her naked body, between her ass cheeks. The shampoo washing off her sharp face and down her neck. I have to do everything in my power to stop myself approaching her. She turns, and I drop to the floor before she can see me.

'Hello,' she says. 'Ammi?'

She must have heard me. I scurry back through the bedroom door, into the hall, just as Ammi is coming out of her room. Now I am behind the sofa in the TV room and this is where I wait until Dilini goes into Maria's room in just her towel. Then she is back in the hall. 'Were you in my room, Ammi?'

'No, darling, I just woke up.'

'Why the hell did you turn the AC off in Maria's room?' she asks. 'I told you I'd pay the electricity if –'

'I didn't. I swear.'

'You're going bloody senile. I took ages getting the temperature right and I went in just now and it was off.'

'It wasn't me,' Ammi says. 'I was asleep.'

'And why the hell did you put pillows in her cot? I told you that's dangerous. And lying Maria on her front, why?'

'I didn't do that, I swear. Even though I don't agree with your western nonsense –'

'She's my baby, okay?' Dilini says.

'I know what I'm doing,' Ammi says. 'You turned out okay, no?'

'Have your own baby and do what you want with it, but with mine, you listen to me or I'm moving out.'

'I haven't been in there, I swear,' Ammi says. 'But I think I saw someone in my room too.'

'Oh come on, Ammi, you always say that. Too much bloody medication.'

Dilini struts away so fast that her towel slips off and I get another glimpse of her beautiful backside but turn before I see more than I should.

Tonight, I am back and I have to wait in the junk room while Ammi and Dilini have yet another argument.

'Bubs, how was the biryani?' Ammi asks.

'What are you on about now, lady?'

'Having said you didn't want it,' Ammi laughs, 'you whacked it.'

'Whacked what?' Dilini asks.

'The biryani. Was it good?'

'Ammi, for all that is good and true please believe me. I did not whack your biryani. The meat's about twenty-five-years old.'

'Look at this,' Ammi says. 'The container is empty and back in the fridge. If you didn't whack it then I'm telling you, there is someone else in this house.'

'I think you could be right,' Dilini says. 'And her name is Goldilocks.'

After they both go to bed I decide to sleep in Baby Maria's nursery, because she is the only one not in a bad mood. Before that, I go to Dilini's room, while she's out cold, to turn the monitor off so that she won't be woken by my singing. I am so tempted to get on top of Dilini and breathe her in, but come on, that's not why I'm here. I'm a daddy now and mummy needs her sleep.

Little Maria wakes up crying for milk, and I know what to do because I have read the formula packaging. I mix five ounces of water with five scoops of powder and shake the bottle furiously. *Don't worry, babe, I'm not an idiot.* I know that the water has to be boiled, and I know the boiled water is in the thermos flask. I use a sterilized bottle too.

Maria's in safe hands.

She sits on my lap looking into my eyes as I put the bottle to her mouth. When she has finished, I know I have to burp her so I carry her on my shoulder for as long as she needs, but when she starts crying, I start singing. I wonder if Dilini will mind if I sing in Sinhala. Often these high-class people think it is beneath them to speak in anything but English.

When Maria is back asleep, I wash the bottle and put it in the sterilizer. Then I go down to the front gate and put a brown envelope in the mailbox. In it is a note that says, 'This is a warning so he does not hurt you like he hurt me.' I leave the note unsigned. With the note is a series of photos I have taken of Madu flirting with other women at recent events.

I return to Dilini's room and put the monitor back on. I lie next to her, my hands to myself, because it would be odd to touch her while she is asleep.

I am under the bed when I hear Dilini scream.

'Oh my God.' She runs to Maria's room. 'Ammi, Ammi.'

I hear doors opening and closing. 'What is it?' Ammi asks. 'What is it?'

That's such an Ammi thing to ask, I think. While they are in Maria's room I sprint down the stairs and into the guestroom, but with the door open, I can still hear them.

'Ammi, please, tell me –'

'Darling, why are you holding me so tight?'

'Please, please you have to think,' Dilini says. 'Did you go into Maria's room at all last night?'

'No, I am pretty sure I didn't.'

'Can you at least tell me this? Did you give her any milk?'

'Definitely not.'

'Oh my God, I can't believe it.' I hear Dilini dropping to the floor.

'Is Maria okay?' Ammi asks.

'Yes, yes,' Dilini says. 'She's breathing, she's sleeping, she's perfect.'

'So what's wrong?'

'Nothing. That's the point. Nothing. I think we now have a baby who sleeps through the night.'

'Are you serious?'

'This is amazing. Absolutely amazing. Now I can start getting my life back on track. Now I can get into shape.'

I hear her running down the stairs and then watch her go to the front gate to collect the post. She starts opening the brown envelope I left there last night while at the same time making a phone call.

My phone rings. Oh God!

'What was that?' she calls out. 'Ammi, is your phone ringing?'

I cut the call before the sound gets any louder. I text Dilini back. 'Sorry madam, cud not answer your call as I am at workout.'

'That's okay,' she replies. 'I have some amazing news. Session, day after tomorrow at 10.30?'

When Dilini arrives at the gym she high-fives me with great conviction, then starts stretching. 'Ready for me to become your favourite and most hardworking client?'

'Surely yes, Madam.'

'My baby has slept through two nights in a row.'

Of course she has, princess.

'Now you're going to see me every single day.'

As if I don't already.

'And we can get rid of these.' She grips the little fat she has under her arms.

'I can barely see it.'

She holds my chin and scrunches up her nose. 'You're so damn sweet and innocent. Why can't all men be like you?'

'They don't do squats.' I pull her arms behind her back to stretch her triceps.

'Can I rely on you to help me change my life around?'

I nod.

'I have two requests.' She leans forward and whispers into my ear. 'Please make sure you plan my workouts so I never bump into that creep Madu again.'

'No problem, Madam. And the second?'

'Whatever it takes, get me the perfect body even if you have to chase, hound, follow me and force me.'

The Dog Thrown off a Building

Udeni Kapuge has stared at the black screen for over an hour. The white writing on it says: 'Video contains footage some viewers may find upsetting.' She holds her breath and presses play, covering her eyes with her hands. A man talks in Sinhala. A dog howls.

This video was posted on Facebook by Embark, the street dog charity at which Udeni volunteers. Now everyone on social media is talking about it. Udeni is aware that some people are searching for the dog while others are tracking down the evil bastard in the video. Yet, two hours later she has still not watched it without covering her eyes.

Twenty-seven years before this video emerged on social media, when Udeni Kapuge was seventeen and unmarried, she had a baby boy. Two months later, her parents put him up for adoption. Ever since, Udeni replays in her head daily the visuals of the Buddhist monk taking him away. It is like a video she cannot pause, and neither can she cover her eyes.

Udeni's parents left her a vast fortune because even though her father accused her of being a slut for tempting an older relative, she was their only slut. She does not spend much of the money, just in case her son finds her. He will need it more. Yet, because of her wealth she can work for free teaching physical movement at a special-needs school, where many kids go to hide from the rest of society. Like Ashan.

Ashan is from a middle-class family. His father is a banker and his mother a teacher. When he is three years old, he becomes obsessed with stacking tins. Every day, he goes straight to the kitchen cupboard and pulls everything out. He stacks obsessively for hours. His parents enrol him in a leading international school, where, aged seven, he makes it his goal to know every single student's birthday off by heart. It takes him one day. Yet, he cannot score more than 10% on any of his assignments and he shows no interest in making friends. The school flags this with Ashan's parents who, in turn, threaten the school with legal action if they label their son with a special-needs tag. Udeni is called in because it is thought that, by teaching physical movement to Ashan, his parents will be none the wiser that she has experience of children with Asperger's Syndrome. She thinks she is making progress when Ashan shows a particular fascination for cricket, but it turns out he is more interested in learning the stats than actually playing. He shows a similar preference for washing machine serial numbers over clean clothes.

In time, Udeni makes a meaningful breakthrough. Ashan becomes obsessed with rock music, and he gets his exercise by mimicking the dances in rock videos. When he is nine, Udeni encourages him to take part in a school talent show, and she is surprised when he accepts the challenge. He will perform in front of two hundred junior school students and three hundred and fifty parents including his own. He refuses to tell Udeni what he is going to do.

When the Extracurricular Head invites Ashan onto the stage, he gets the biggest cheer of the afternoon by far. He wears trousers, cut off just below the knees, and a blood-red bandana on his head. He takes his white t-shirt off. Some of the other kids snigger in the audience and point at his man boobs. When backing music comes on, Ashan hangs his head, and taps his feet. When the beat starts, he sprints across the stage and jumps against the wall. Out comes the air guitar, out comes his tongue. He begins to sing – some would say scream. The problem is, every other lyric is some form of the F word and this is for an audience of children aged three to eleven. The Extracurricular Head dives at the speaker and pulls out the wires, but that only makes Ashan sing louder. Parents run forward to pick up their children, covering their ears.

Ashan keeps going, possibly having the best or the worst time of his life, no one can tell.

Ashan's parents sneak out of the auditorium. Udeni realizes it is incumbent on her to get Ashan off the stage. Ashan ignores her. He keeps going until the end of the song, and when he finishes, calm as you like, he bows and puts his white t-shirt back on.

Udeni takes Ashan to an empty classroom. He asks her, 'Why did nobody clap even though I tried so hard?'

The next day Ashan's parents enrol him full-time at the special-needs school but they never pick him up or drop him off themselves. Udeni guesses it is their way of denying it all. If people know they have a special needs son, they will wonder what he did in a previous life to deserve such bad karma. They will wonder what they did to deserve such a son.

Ashan's condition does not worsen, nor does it get better. He has the ability to communicate well with other students, but not the inclination to do so. Udeni knows that the two things she can't do is hug him or wake him up from his random naps, which he takes anywhere he can find silence.

After a full day's work at the school, Udeni is at her computer again. She looks at the on-screen scan of a faded photograph of her baby son. She pours herself a glass of wine and presses play on the video.

The camera focuses on an overweight man with a moustache, wearing a white shirt and a large shiny watch. He holds a brown-and-black dog by the skin on its neck and back. The dog is standing on the concrete ledge of what looks to be a six-storey building. In the background there is lush vegetation.

Udeni takes a deep breath.

The video is now in slow motion. The camera is pointed down towards the ground, then back up again as the man lifts the dog off the ledge and puts him back down again, perhaps because the cameraman tells him he is not ready.

The camera pans out a little, taking in the man's face. He is smiling so much that the white of his teeth complements the white of his shirt. He stares down at ground level once again, and then back at the camera.

The dog's tail is wagging, although part of it is tucked between its legs.

The man lifts the dog, and with a flourish throws it in the air. He holds the pose of his follow-through. The black-and-brown dog, legs spread wide, appears to be floating because the video is in slow motion. Its body is bending back and forth from the middle. It sounds like the dog is shouting 'Aiyo' as if bemoaning its fate as it falls through the sky.

The cameraman loses the visual of the dog, but captures the audio of it screaming. The visual and audio are back in sync for the dog's landing on a thick green undergrowth.

Udeni cries. Like the noise of the tuktuk taking away her baby son, she knows she will relive, a million times over, the thud and screams of the dog when it lands.

The dog moves a little before the video ends.

As with her baby son, there is hope.

Embark's celebrity owner, Otara, makes a social media plea to find this dog. Udeni is on the frontlines. There are a lot of other good people and the dog is found.

Otara asks Udeni to name him.

She names him Aiyo.

It takes three months to get Aiyo walking again. Even with Otara, Udeni and most of the other dog lovers in the country, Aiyo shows a distinct lack of trust and who can blame him? Udeni asks if she can keep him. After Embark release him in her garden, he rarely comes out of the bushes. Udeni stays at home all week with Aiyo, never leaving him. She places food outside for him and watches from upstairs as he comes out to eat it as quickly as possible before scurrying back into the bushes.

Eventually Udeni has to go back to work, but she refuses to leave Aiyo alone so she uses all her animal-handling training to catch him. Aiyo tries to bite her when she grabs him by the skin on the back of his neck, but in due course he calms down and allows her to put him in the back of her car.

She takes him to the special-needs school where he is kept in a fenced-off play area. Udeni goes about her work. Later, she comes out to check on Aiyo, but sees Ashan lying on his back on the slide.

'Ashan,' she calls out to him. 'Ashan.'

Aiyo is next to Ashan. Udeni is about to run in to protect Ashan, or to protect Aiyo – she is not sure who is in greater danger.

Aiyo leans over Ashan.

'No, Aiyo, no,' Udeni shouts.

Aiyo licks Ashan's face, waking him up. No one wakes up Ashan. Ashan sits up and Aiyo runs back to the bushes. Udeni opens the gates to the play area so that she can go in to get Ashan but she stops because Ashan has his hand out towards Aiyo. He makes kissing noises and then claps.

Aiyo's head appears out of the bush, then he edges forward, his nose pointed down, his tail wagging like crazy. He allows Ashan to stroke his head before running off back to the bushes again.

When the school bell rings, Udeni takes half an hour trying to catch Aiyo so that she can take him home. The next day, however, Aiyo is waiting by her car to come to work with her. After a few weeks, Udeni allows Aiyo to roam freely around school and he is friendly with all of the students. He follows Ashan. Everywhere.

Sometimes Udeni takes them both for walks. When they come back, Ashan has his bottle of water next to Aiyo's bowl. When Ashan has his nap, Aiyo is always by his side. When there is thunder and lightning, Aiyo lies on top of Ashan and they both whimper in their own ways.

Ashan is now sixteen years old. No one knows Aiyo's age.

After a long weekend, Udeni brings Aiyo to school and there is no Ashan. Aiyo follows Udeni everywhere, but is not himself.

Udeni calls Ashan's parents and they tell him he passed away in his sleep two nights earlier. Then they put down the phone.

There is no funeral.

There is no obituary in the papers.

Udeni asks for help from the Embark team and soon they have found Ashan's grave in an overcrowded, lopsided cemetery just outside Colombo and not far from Udeni's house. His grave stands out from the others because it is well-maintained, and surrounded by flowers. The marble gravestone reads:

Ashan Ranjan Joseph Pennaboke
2nd April 1995 – 13th July 2011
There shall be no darkness,
Nor dazzling,
But one equal light
No noise, nor silence
Just your beautiful life song
And we are all clapping this time.

Udeni walks Aiyo every Saturday and they end up at Ashan's grave. She speaks to the graveyard watcher who only works at night. He says every evening Ashan's parents come to sit at Ashan's grave, and cry. They do not like anyone seeing them there.

A few weeks pass and Aiyo becomes more and more unpredictable. He has started growling, with bared teeth, at any visitor to the school except for the children. One day he bites a student's mother and there is a police report filed against the school. Udeni can no longer bring him to work.

Today there is an almighty storm and Udeni sits at school worrying about Aiyo because she has locked him out in the garden. There is shelter on the veranda, but with the winds as they are Aiyo must be soaked by now. Udeni waits for the final school bell and drives home, but because parts of Colombo are flooded it takes her more than an hour. When she parks the car, she jumps out in the rain and calls for Aiyo. She notices a hole dug under the back gate.

She knows, from past experience, that he must be running from the thunder thinking it is chasing him. She looks for him, in the lightning and torrential rain, for seven hours. To begin with, it is just her, but soon she is joined by builders from construction sites, tuktuk drivers, neighbours. People let Udeni into their houses to call Aiyo's name, they feed her and carry her in the back of pick-up tricks, holding umbrellas above her head. The animal charities get involved, at which point they insist Udeni go to sleep. The next morning she finds out that the search party did not stop looking all night, reaffirming her faith in humanity. It is still bucketing it down with rain.

Udeni has a thought but she cannot share it with the others because they will think she is crazy. She puts on her trainers, black leggings and a fluorescent yellow Nike tank top. She jogs to the graveyard where Ashan is buried.

As soon as she arrives she senses something, but she doesn't know what. The rain has abated but the air is heavy with water lifting off the warming asphalt of the road and there is a smell of doused-out smoke from a bonfire which must have been lit in the lull between the storms. Udeni opens the gate and looks at the ground as she walks, ensuring that she does not trample on any other graves and when she comes to Ashan's, she knows she will see Aiyo.

But he is not there. She waits with Ashan for a few seconds but cannot sit still so she heads back towards the gate.

Aiyo is standing at the fence barking. He can't get in. There are police sirens in the background.

'Aiyo,' Udeni shouts out. She smiles, but only for a few seconds. Up the road a woman on a big black motorcycle crashes into a green tuktuk. A red jeep flashes by.

Like in the video she watched, Udeni hears a thud and a dog's howl, but this time she cannot press pause or cover her eyes with her hands.

Everyone Has to Eat

PASINDU AMARASINGHE IS a closet homosexual with six toes on his left foot, but the one thing he never wants his friends to find out is that he's been allocated a university application fee waiver. It's no secret he's on scholarship at Colombo's most exclusive school and that he lives with his mother in a one-room annex to a poor man's house, but he refuses to walk around with his hands cupped asking for handouts. Like everyone else, he's paying for his damn applications.

So while his friends are spending the summer holidays building their CVs by taking on unpaid internships at Lanka Hospitals and the Supreme Court, Pasindu's relying on tips to be able to pay for his seven university applications. He waits tables at a niche cafe named after Aiyo, a dog made famous for being thrown off a six-storey building and surviving. It is styled like an English tea room, with floral armchairs, wooden floors, chandeliers, and a life-size dollhouse. Because it is small and intimate, within its four walls there are no secrets, and what happens in Aiyo does not stay in Aiyo.

Pasindu's become a bit of a master at knowing which tables to serve for the best tip. Muttiah Muralitharan is the highest wicket-taker in the history of test cricket, but he also talks a hell of a lot so takes up a lot of time. Yet, he's a damn nice guy and, more importantly, he's a fantastic tipper, so it's worth it. Singers Bathiya and Santhush are always together, and they each give ten per cent meaning Pasindu gets twenty, so if they ever come in he makes sure he's playing their music on the cafe sound system.

The staff do not share tips with each other, so they tend to fight over the biggest spenders. This is why Pasindu is pissed off when his boss tells him to wait a table occupied by a security guard and his son. The guard is in khaki trousers tucked into knee-length socks, a mauve beret, a white shirt with a black tie and a grey jacket with mock medals sewn onto it. His son is in the standard white bleached uniform of government-run schools, but his trousers are at least two inches too short for him, so his dust-stained socks sit limply over his battered plimsolls. Pasindu guesses he is about nine years old.

The table they pick only seats two, so Pasindu cannot rightfully ask them to leave. It is next to a window, outside which the son has parked a bicycle which is painted in police blue. The father removes his beret and blows on its metal badge, before rubbing it against his shirt. He shoves away cutlery and sauce bottles so that he has space, bang in the middle of the table, for the damn thing. He spits on his palm and flattens down his comb-over before breathing in deeply through his untrimmed nostril hairs. He clicks his finger at Pasindu, makes a kissing sound and says, 'Malli, malli, menu card, menu card.'

Pasindu's first reaction is to say, *I am not your malli. I have 11 A*s at IGCSE, and I'm taking four A Levels.* Instead he bites his tongue. There is something about this country – people don't talk about caste, snobbery or hierarchy, but a security guard calling over a waiter with a click of his fingers? Pasindu ignores the guard and goes to the kitchen counter, pretending to place an order.

'Malli, malli,' the guard says. 'Did you hear me? Menu cards, please.'

Rolling his eyes, Pasindu backs away towards his boss. 'Should I ask them to leave?'

The boss writes down some numbers. 'Just give them a menu,' he says. 'Let's see what they order.'

'How do we know they'll be able to pay, sir?'

The boss puts a hand on Pasindu's shoulder in an I-am-your-boss-even-if-I-may-be-one-of-you kind of way. 'Let's see what they order.'

Pasindu approaches the guard's table, making sure he breathes through his mouth because either the guard or his son smells musty and pungent. He gives them one menu to share. 'Can you read English?'

The guard sits up straight. 'Since I studied in

Shakespeare College, Kandy, I can insure you that my English is too good, thank you very much.'

'Okay,' Pasindu says. 'I must point out that we are a small restaurant, and everyone has to eat if they want to keep a table.'

'Malli, that's why we're here,' the guard says, switching to Sinhala. He opens the menu and pushes it towards his son.

'Thathi,' the son asks, 'what is a nasi goreng?'

'Show me where,' the guard says. 'Ah, goreng is surely a German dish.'

'Wow,' the son says. 'You know everything.'

'And it is a form of sausage,' the guard says.

'It's rice,' Pasindu says.

'Or sometimes it is rice,' the guard says.

'Okay I will have that, Thathi.'

'Good choice, putha.' The guard takes out his wallet, which is bulging at the seams and filled with bills. He grabs Pasindu's arm and leans into him. He points at the menu. 'This says one thousand six hundred rupees. That is the cost of one nazi goreng?'

'Nasi,' Pasindu says.

'What?'

Pasindu nods his head. 'Yes, the cost of one. If it's too much ...'

'No, no. I was just surprised it was so cheap. Must I add tax and service charge to this price?'

'No, sir ...'

'Call me Jinesena.'

'No, sir, as you can see at the bottom of the menu, everything is included in the price.'

'Oh so you don't get any service charge?'

Pasindu fakes a smile. 'Any gratuity is at the discretion of the customer.'

'I see,' the guard says.

'What does that mean, Thathi?'

Jinesena starts counting the money in his wallet. 'Putha, do you want anything else?'

'Like a drink?' the son asks.

'Yes, please, please have a drink ... if you must.'

'Can I have iced tea?'

'Of course you can, birthday boy.' The guard looks at the menu and then at an increasingly impatient Pasindu. 'Oh Jesus. That is seven hundred and fifty?'

'Is that too much for you, sir?'

'Of course not. Mere pocket change.'

'Oh, I'm sorry,' Pasindu says. 'I thought I heard you say Jesus.'

'I did, because you see, that is my son's name.'

'Thathi, my name is Nalaka!'

'That's your surname. Jesus is your Christian name.'

'What are you talking, Thathi?'

Lifting a finger to his lips, Jinesena says, 'So iced tea is seven hundred and fifty?'

Nodding, Pasindu wonders how much money he could be earning if he was serving the gorgeous hunk with the John Travolta *Pulp Fiction* hairstyle who just walked in wearing head-to-toe Versace. The waitress on duty ties up her hair and pats down her apron as she takes his order.

'But a hot tea is only four hundred, no?' Jinesena asks, without Pasindu noticing.

'I can have hot tea if you want, Thathi,' Nalaka says. 'And we can let it cool.'

'Don't be silly, putha. You have anything you want. No son of mine has to deny himself a ...'

'So I'll have a hot chocolate pudding also, Thathi?'

'Don't be greedy, putha.' Jinesena counts his money again, and takes out his phone.

'What about for you, sir?' Pasindu asks him.

'One thousand six hundred, plus seven hundred and fifty, is two thousand three fifty. I wouldn't mind having the lamprais but it says one thousand three hundred.'

'Okay, one lamprais,' Pasindu says.

'Just a second. Malli, can you bring pen and paper, please?'

Pasindu looks towards the boss who points to a pad of paper.

'Maths has always been my strength,' Jinesena says.

'He could have been a Maths professor,' Nalaka adds.

'But he chose to be a security guard instead?' replies Pasindu.

'Not any security guard. Thathi is Deputy Sergeant of the Monsoon Lodge Security Unit.'

Pasindu clicks his feet together and salutes. 'I'm so sorry,' he says through his teeth. 'I didn't realize I was in the presence of an officer.'

Jinesena salutes back. 'One second,' he says, with a finger pointed up in Pasindu's direction. 'Malli, do you have any special items that are not on the menu?'

'Yes, sir.'

'Music to my ears,' he says.

'But they're more expensive.'

'And I don't like music,' Jinesena says. 'You see, I really just want a small bite.' He slaps his stomach. 'Must watch the old pot, no?'

'So something cheaper, perhaps?' Pasindu asks, under his breath.

'Well, I forgot my credit cards. All of them. There's American Express, Visa, Master.' He smiles inanely. 'All at home in my blue-colour trouser.'

'Thathi, I have some money,' Nalaka says.

'Don't be silly. It's your birthday.' The guard laughs and waves his arms, as if volleying the suggestion away. 'How much?'

'Exactly fifty rupees.'

'Oh.'

'Sir, I have to serve other customers. Shall I just place an order for your son's items for now, although I must remind you that to keep the table everybody has to eat.'

'I will look at the menu again,' he says.

'Thathi, the lamprais is the cheapest main course on the menu.'

'Oh yes, so it is.' Jinesena counts his money again and writes something down, before grabbing Pasindu's arm a second time. 'Is it possible to give me a small lamprais for one thousand?'

'No,' Pasindu says.

'What about a lamprais without the egg and the cutlet?'

'I am sorry but ...'

'How about if you remove the banana leaf and the seeni sambol, and also the chicken?'

Still shaking his head even though he is no longer listening, Pasindu smiles at Versace Travolta, subconsciously hiding his six-toed foot behind his other leg, even though he is wearing covered shoes.

'What if you remove the ash plantain and the wambatu moju?' Jinesena asks.

'Then you would just be left with yellow rice.'

'Which is exactly what I want.'

'Fine, but our prices are fixed.' Pasindu puts the pad in his shirt pocket. 'I would still have to charge you the one thousand three hundred.'

Jinesena stands and holds Pasindu's right hand in both of his. 'This is so embarrassing as normally I carry at least half a lakh with me, but today, alas, I need to have something for one thousand.'

'You could have the warm chocolate pudding, Thathi,' his son says. 'And we could share everything.'

Jinesena lifts the menus and hands them to Pasindu. 'The nazi, the iced tea and the warm chocolate, please. Taxes are included, no?'

'Yes, sir.'

'And there is no service charge?'

Pasindu doesn't bother answering that last question. He leaves the guard's order at the kitchen before strutting past Versace Travolta and through the swing door onto the main road. He completes a few standing press-ups against the wall to pump blood into his muscles, and then uses the window's reflection to check whether he is presentable enough to approach Versace Travolta. Satisfied that he looks as good as he can in a cafe apron, he returns inside.

'Thathi,' Nalaka asks, 'do you think the iced tea has milk and sugar in it?'

The guard rubs his belly and laughs. 'Of course, putha, how can they serve any tea without milk and sugar?'

'I don't know, Thathi, but this place is so confusing.'

'Don't talk bloody nonsense, putha.'

'For this money we could eat for weeks at Hotel de Zam Zam.'

'It is your birthday, putha, and I told you I would spare no expense.'

'But neighbour Dilshan said that we should know our place also, no?'

Jinesena moves his chair around so that he has his back to everyone else in the cafe. 'You know Ganga the elephant at Gangaramaya Temple?'

'Yes, Thathi.'

'He is chained at the ankle. Do you think he cannot break those chains?'

'No, Thathi, because if he could, he would run free.'

'Putha, he is a three-thousand-kilogram beast. He could break the shackles with a mere kick.'

'Then why doesn't he?'

'Because he has been chained since he was a small baby. As a baby he could not break the chains. As a toddler he could not break those chains so soon he gave up trying. Now he believes he still can't break free.'

'Ah, I see, Thathi,' says Nalaka.

'Do you, putha?'

'Not so much.'

Jinesena stretches his arm around the room, stopping at Versace Travolta who is paying for a cup of coffee with a five-thousand-rupee note. 'Putha, we may be spending a bit less than others, but it is with the same money made of paper like everyone else's.'

'Yet after this meal we will have nothing left.'

'You are wrong, my boy. We have our eyes and our hands and legs, so we can always make more money.' He points outside. 'And we have your bicycle.'

'You're not going to try to sell it again, are you?'

'The bike given to us by Cuckoo Siva, the most powerful man in the country, because I saved his son? I wouldn't even dream about it, putha.'

Pasindu serves the iced tea with a scowl no customer deserves, but he can't help himself. Versace Travolta has left the waitress a two-hundred rupee tip, and soon he will be off before Pasindu has had the chance to talk to him.

Nalaka sips his iced tea. 'I thought you said it would have milk in it.'

'I thought I said that too,' Jinesena says. 'But obviously we were both mistaken.' He picks up a newspaper from the rack next to their table and starts to read. 'Drink, drink, putha.'

Pasindu serves the nasi goreng to Jinesena, who moves the plate towards his son, and then tucks napkins into both their shirts. Nalaka is about to use his hands to ball up the rice, but Jinesena grabs him by the wrists. 'These kind of people eat everything with fork and spoon.'

Nalaka picks up the cutlery as if holding two pens. He wolfs down a big bite.

Jinesena waves to Pasindu. 'Malli, come here please.' He turns to his son. 'Now say thank you to the waiter.'

'Thank you,' the son calls out.

Pasindu fakes a smile and wanders off.

'Putha, you do not judge a man's worth by the size of his car, but by his manners.' He points at the nasi goreng. 'How is it?'

'It is like a dream, Thathi. This is my best birthday ever.'

'That's all I want for you. But why are you wearing such a frown on your face?'

'I am worried that because of my birthday you will fall into debt again.'

'I promise I won't,' Jinesena says. 'Besides, I have found Jesus and the man who is his mouthpiece and best friend runs a church near my work. We will never be left wanting again.'

Jinesena wipes chocolate sauce off his son's face and then calls for the bill. Pasindu calculates that he owes three thousand three hundred and fifty rupees, and assumes that the guard will fall short. However, the boss told him to accept whatever Jinesena gives, because Sanga and Mahela are on their way and want that specific table by the window. They are the best tippers around.

Jinesena opens the bill folder and, without looking, drops every penny he has into it, including the coins his son gave him. He tips his beret towards Pasindu and to the other customers and ambles outside to unchain his son's bike.

It takes Pasindu a few seconds to stack up the coins and sort through the crumpled notes but he notices that Jinesena has miscalculated and left three hundred and thirty-five rupees too much. Pasindu looks around the cafe as if to check if anyone would notice if he pocketed this extra money, but finds himself running outside and shouting to Jinesena. Nalaka, seemingly used to his father being in trouble, tries to make a run for it but the guard catches him by his frayed collar.

Pasindu hands Jinesena the folder.

'What's wrong? What's wrong?' he asks.

'You left too much money,' Pasindu says. 'You could have had the lamprais after all. Maybe it's a good thing you didn't become a Maths professor.'

Jinesena smiles as he tucks his trousers back into his long socks and straightens his beret. 'The bill was three thousand three hundred and fifty, no?'

'It says so right here.' Pasindu points to the bottom line. 'You could have had the whole shebang. Yellow rice, cutlet, ash plantain, wambatu moju, seeni sambol.'

'And the chicken?' Jinesena asks.

'And the chicken,' Pasindu says.

'I love chicken.' Jinesena licks his lips and closes his eyes. 'But I also know that waiters rely on tips to make ends meet.'

'What was that?' Pasindu asks.

Jinesena smiles. 'The total was three thousand three hundred and fifty, of which ten percent is three hundred and thirty-five, which is exactly what I left for you, because, malli, everybody has to eat.'

Help, Help

KIYOMA HAS BEEN on her feet for all of the seven hours since lunch, barring the twenty minutes she sat scraping the meat out of coconuts to make pol sambol. It's almost nine in the evening, which means soon she can put her feet up and watch TV. Last night the teledrama she is hooked on ended in great suspense. With a rich husband and two beautiful kids, Geetha has the perfect life, but who is her real father?

Balancing herself precariously above the squatting pan, Kiyoma takes a quick shower. She squeezes into her bedroom, placing her TV on her stomach while she nibbles on the fish cutlets left over from her boss's lunch party. When the teledrama starts, she fiddles with the coat-hanger antenna to improve the picture quality. She wishes she could share with someone her shock that Manjula is Geetha's brother.

The bell outside her room rings. She moves the TV to one side and crawls out of bed. 'Coming, Madam.'

Upstairs, she stands at the door to the family room. Madam is wearing short shorts, her legs hairless and long. Kiyoma envies Madam's fair skin and soft, straight hair and thinks she looks much better just before bed, when she is not caked in make-up. Umalie, Madam's daughter, is three years old and weighs the same as her baby brother, Kayaan, who is shaped like a beach ball. Neither can speak much Sinhala, so Kiyoma has been forced to learn to communicate with them through a combination of broken English, high-pitched noises and hand gestures. Soon after the birth of each of her own two children, Kiyoma returned to work in Saudi and her aunt brought them up. Yet, with Madam and Sir's kids, she has bathed, fed and played with them since she started working for the family eighteen months ago.

'Can I have a glass of iced water, please?' Madam asks.

Kiyoma trudges past the upstairs fridge, which she is not supposed to open, and down to the kitchen. On her way back up she passes Sir who is carrying Kayaan and showing him the garden under the lights. As always, she marvels at how alike father and son look, especially when they smile as they both have the kind of dimples that would make them celebrities back in her village. She knows Kayaan will grow, one day, into a handsome and strong man like his father.

She points at Kayaan. 'If you show chooti baba the plants for too long his kaka will become green.'

'We don't believe in such things, do we, Kayaan?' Sir laughs. 'Aiyo, sorry, could you please make me some tea?'

Sir has not been himself recently; usually he has a joke for everything, but these days he has bags under his eyes and is often distant, even with his own kids. Yet, Kiyoma knows that if she told him about her teledrama he would understand and encourage her to get back to it, but she doesn't want to put him in that position.

Although Kiyoma makes it back to her room in time to see the end of the teledrama, when she hears Umalie crying she runs back upstairs, resigned to the fact that she will not know who Geetha's father is till tomorrow.

'I think she had a bad dream,' Madam says.

'You look very tired, Madam.' Kiyoma extends her arms to take Umalie from her. 'I can put her to sleep again.'

Madam smiles. 'Thank you. We have to get her up at seven tomorrow, so please don't let her con you into playing.'

'Don't worry, Madam.' Kiyoma smiles and taps Umalie on the back. 'My Sinhala songs will help her go to bed quickly.'

As soon as Madam leaves the room, Umalie cons Kiyoma into playing hide-and-seek, after which they share a bottle of sugar-coated sweets.

'Don't tell Mummy, okay?' Umalie says in a put-on Sri Lankan accent, before she falls asleep.

'It can be another of our secrets.' Kiyoma rubs her nose against Umalie's and kisses her head. She pops into Kayaan's room and feels his chest to make sure he is breathing. She will miss this routine, and the joy it brings her, when she returns to see her own family in the village next week. Whenever she has gone home in the past – usually once in two months – her kids have tried to stop her from leaving; she used to extend her stays by saying she had a funeral to attend, but Madam stopped pretending to believe her when Kiyoma claimed for a second time that her mother-in-law had died. Yet, returning on time does not bother her. In many ways, she is happier being with Umalie and Kayaan than she is with her own kids. Being back home is about a constant reminder of how difficult it is to bring up children on a maid's salary.

Waking at six, Kiyoma walks Eddie, Sir's adopted street dog, and waters the lawn before the sun comes up. After this, she gets the kids' breakfast ready. She loves feeding Kayaan because he eats so well but Umalie has little interest in food. To save her being told off by Madam, Kiyoma finishes her banana for her.

As is often the case these days, Sir is on the phone, arguing with someone about money. He is out the door and in his silver Audi without remembering to say bye to his kids.

Once the rest of the family leaves, Kiyoma starts cleaning Madam's walk-in wardrobe as instructed, pulling out and dusting all her shoes. She tries on a pair of the highest heels and wonders how on earth Madam can walk in them. After an hour of cleaning, Kiyoma takes a break, sitting at Sir's desk so that she can phone her children. She loves talking to them, but the main purpose of the call is to make sure that they haven't spoken to their father in the last week. Towards the end of each month he travels from the estate on which he plucks coconuts, and hangs out with the kids only so he can call Kiyoma and threaten to hurt them if she doesn't send him money. The kids assure her that he has not been in touch, so she is able to relax a little, before she starts ironing everything, including washcloths and underpants, as per Madam's instructions

When Madam returns home with the kids she looks in the fridge. 'Where is the Kit Kat sir bought the other day for Umalie?'

'I never saw it,' Kiyoma says which is not entirely true. She did see it, but she didn't take it. Sure she helps herself to a treat here and there, but only if no one else seems to be eating them. She definitely wouldn't take something of Umalie's.

'Are you quite sure?'

'I don't even know what Kit Kat is, Madam.' This is another unnecessary lie, but sometimes Kiyoma can't help herself because she is accused of so many things.

'Okay then,' Madam says under her breath. 'There must be a ghost in the house, I guess.'

Later, when Kiyoma empties the kitchen bin she finds the Kit Kat wrapper along with the empty cans of cider Madam had with her two friends at lunch the day before.

The next day, Kiyoma wakes to the chants of Buddhist monks from the temple up the road. She is excited because it is kukal mas day – once a week Madam lets her have chicken with her vegetable curry.

For once, Sir stops on his way out to work. 'I've left a box of toys outside your room. Maybe your kids will like them.'

'Thank you, Sir, but what about Umalie and Kayaan?'

'We don't think they're safe for them.' Sir looks away. 'Someone gave them to us for Umalie but, I mean, they're made in China and Madam thinks, um, you know ...'

'Thank you, sir.'

She knows Sir's intentions are good and this reminds her that she has to buy him a present for his birthday tomorrow. She wants to give him something special because he came to her rescue last time her husband came to try to beat her – although he did warn her that a repeat episode could lead to her losing her job because of the potential risks to Umalie and Kayaan.

Madam allows her to go out shopping, as long as she catches up on all her chores when she comes back – even if it means working late tonight. Kiyoma knows that Sir takes great pride in his collection of sunglasses so she goes to Pettah market and finds him a pair that can fold into a small circle. She also finds her daughter a Carbie Doll which is like a chubby version of Umalie's Barbie, and a Mickey the Mouse Umbrella for Umalie, a rattle toy for Kayaan, and a skirt and some underwear for herself.

When she gives Sir his sunglasses, he holds his hand to his heart and says, 'You really should not have spent so much on these.' He is wearing them when the family head out for his birthday treat.

Soon Kiyoma's husband is hammering at the gate. 'Open quickly, quickly, now.'

Kiyoma places each of her palms around the iron grills of the gate. 'Go away, man, Sir is home.'

'Don't talk rot, woman. I saw him leave just now. Let me in or I shall shout so loud the neighbours will hear and when they tell your bloody bastard Sir that I have come, he will surely kick your ass out his house and all the way back to Bandarawela.'

'Sir has cameras.'

'Well, if he ever checked them, he would know that I have been outside a number of times to see if I can call your name.'

'What do you want this time?' Kiyoma asks, unlocking the gate.

'I have a bloody sure-fire horse running in two hours. We will be so beauty rich we won't know what to do with our wealth.'

'I have no money.'

He pushes her aside so he can come through the gate. 'You think I am a fool? It is salary day.'

'Yes, but I took so many advances and also went shopping to Pettah yesterday.'

'You spent all your children's money on this crap?' He yanks Kiyoma's ankle-length skirt up to her waist. 'Even these jungies don't look cheap.' He pulls her in towards his chest, his hands under her blouse, before he shoves her against the gate. 'You know I have to win this bet.'

'Or Leg-Breaker Gunesekera will kill you?'

'Something like that.' He gets on his tiptoes to peer through the head-to-toe glass on the upstairs landing. 'Umalie and Kayaan's rooms are up there, no?'

'Don't you dare!'

'They're growing so fast.'

She is used to her husband threatening their own kids, but she knows deep down he loves them. She has no idea of what he might be capable of with someone else's kids. 'Let me look in my room and see what I can find for you,' she says.

'No, I'll look.' He strides up the twenty-metre driveway, lined with stunted palm trees, and into Kiyoma's bedroom. He throws everything about and she fears that he will find her secret shoe box under the bed and that will be the end of it. Sure enough he does and he carries it with its lid off as he marches back towards her, kicking her to the ground. He pours the photographs in the box on top of her, scrunching up a few of them in her mouth. He holds her nose. 'You're a pathetic woman. Pathetic.'

She pushes his hands away from her mouth and nose so she can breathe.

'How much do you want?'

He returns to the room and comes out with the TV.

'That's Sir's,' says Kiyoma. 'He'll track you down and kill you if you take it.'

He laughs. 'Do you think I'm scared of that bloody bastard?'

'Yes.'

'I'll pawn it and return it in three hours after I win.' He lifts it in the air and examines it further. 'This is a cheap piece of shit. I'll need another two thousand at least.'

'I don't have any cash.'

'Then I'll find something else of theirs to take.'

He stomps towards the main house, but Kiyoma stands in front of him, back-pedalling as he pushes her. She trips and he gets on top of her, pulling out the box-cutter he always carries. He sits on her chest, drawing blood from her neck – just enough to scare, not enough to kill. She promises to give him two thousand rupees which she takes from Umalie's piggy bank.

Then he is gone, but she is left holding her neck to stop the blood. She collects all the photographs and lays them on the hot stones of the driveway, trying to iron out the creases. She puts them back in her shoe box before washing the blood off her neck with the garden hose. Upstairs, she takes a plaster from the linen cupboard, using it to stop the bleeding so that she will not stain Madam's clothes when she irons.

She finishes all her assigned jobs – at least the ones Madam will be able to notice, although she does not waste time sweeping under the sofa. Tomorrow she will ask Sir for another small advance on her salary so she can replace the money in Umalie's piggy bank.

When their car pulls in through the gates and up the driveway, Sir is wearing his old sunglasses, not the ones she had given him. Madam gets the kids to their rooms and then goes around the house checking Kiyoma's work. She calls her upstairs, which Kiyoma knows is not a good sign. In the beginning, Madam loved to praise her in front of everyone who would listen, but now she will do so in passing, and under her breath if at all.

When Kiyoma gets to the landing, Madam is standing by the linen cupboard. Holding the first-aid kit, she looks at Kiyoma's neck with great concern. For a second, it seems like she is worried about her maid's well-being.

'Did you take a plaster from here?' Madam leans in so close Kiyoma can feel her breath on her skin.

'No, Madam.'

'Then what is that on your neck?'

'A plaster, Madam.'

'And where did you get it?'

'Arpico, Madam.'

Madam pulls a box out of her pocket. 'These are Dora the Explorer plasters. I got them in Malaysia, because as you should know, Umalie is obsessed with Dora. You did not get that plaster from Aprico because you cannot buy these there.'

'Madam, maybe it was another shop.'

'You cannot buy them anywhere in this country.'

Not knowing what to say, Kiyoma smiles and wobbles her head.

'This is not funny,' Madam says. 'Please stop smiling.' She turns and marches to her room. 'Wait downstairs.'

While Sir and Madam argue in their bedroom, Kiyoma stands in the sitting room, waiting. Moments later, Madam comes downstairs and hands her the bottle of sweets from Umalie's room. 'I bought these eight days ago,' she says. 'Now I am guessing you think they're just sweets, but they're vitamins. I give Umalie two a day, so there should only be sixteen missing from this bottle. Shake it.'

Kiyoma does as told.

'Feels pretty empty, no?' She smiles, as if she is pleased with herself. 'Any idea why?'

'Maybe this is the old bottle?' I ask.

'Ah, I did think of that, but you see, if you could read English you would know that these particular vitamins have Omega-3 in them, whereas the last ones I bought didn't. Omega-3 is very good for the brain, by the way.'

Remaining silent, Kiyoma senses that Madam is mocking her.

'These vitamins cost two thousand seven hundred rupees for sixty lozenges. Forty are missing, which is virtually two thousand bucks. That's a lot of money, right?'

'Yes, Madam.'

'So, please do tell me, where are the forty missing vitamins?'

Umalie appears behind her mother holding her hands up in prayer.

'I have no idea.'

'I see,' Madam says. 'Please can you water the garden?'

Kiyoma knows what this means because it has happened a few times in the past, although that was before she had anything as personal as her shoe box to hide. Madam wants Kiyoma out of the house so she can search her room. Kiyoma is going to be caught for a number of things, but if there is a genuine game-changer it will be the shoe box.

By the time Kiyoma returns inside, Madam is sitting at the dining table with a range of items in front of her, but not the shoe box. She starts pointing. 'A container of chicken curry, Tim Tams from Australia, my razors –'

'Madam, you had thrown those in the bin.'

'A present meant for Umalie –'

'– Sir …'

'I gave that to her,' Sir says.

'Did you also give her your spare phone charger?'

Sir ignores the question.

'Because you accused me of losing it, but lo and behold, it was in the maid's room.' Madam turns to face Kiyoma. 'I understand, people have urges. I understand, from time to time, you may want to taste certain things that I have. But you have to ask. You can't just take. Do you understand?'

Kiyoma nods.

'Because this gives me the opportunity to say yes or no. This is your last chance, okay? It really is.'

Kiyoma smiles. 'Thank you, Madam.'

'Wait,' she says. 'Just one more question.'

'Yes, Madam.'

'Where is your TV?'

'It is not there?' Kiyoma asks.

'I took it to be repaired,' Sir says.

As soon as Kiyoma returns to her room, she wriggles under the bed to retrieve her shoe box. The lid is off and eight photographs are missing. All that is left are the photographs of her kids, and the drawings Umalie gave her. Kiyoma is certain Madam did not see the missing photos or she would have asked her to leave on the spot. Someone has though, and Kiyoma knows what to expect. Somehow, she falls asleep.

There is a knock at her door. In one episode of the teledrama Kiyoma watches, Geetha is in a prison cell, until she is summoned to face an executioner. This is how Kiyoma feels, although she doubts she will get a last-minute pardon.

'Can you pack your things, please?' Sir says.

She doesn't ask why. If she did he would tell her that he knows her husband came and took the TV and as long as she works here, there will always be a risk to Umalie and Kayaan. Yet, she knows there is more to it than that. She knows he is the one who has seen the photographs in the shoe box – like the one of her in Madam's wedding dress; or her in Madam's yellow Buddhi Batiks blouse, pretending to breastfeed Kayaan – something Madam never did herself; or the family photo, complete with Eddie in the foreground, with a cut-out of Kiyoma pasted on the side. Worst of all, and perhaps impossible to ignore, the photo of Madam and Sir lounging in bed, but with Madam's head replaced with hers.

Opening the door slightly, Kiyoma looks down at Sir's feet. He hands her a brown envelope. 'You took so many advances your salary is up to date, but here's a little money as a bonus.'

She takes the envelope in two hands and bows. 'Can I say bye to the children?'

'They're fast asleep,' he says. 'So make sure Madam doesn't hear.'

She sneaks up to Kayaan's room first and puts her hand to his chest to make sure he is breathing. She leaves the rattle toy she bought him on his side table. She can taste the salty tears that have rolled down her face into her mouth. She knows if she ever sees this beautiful boy again he will have no idea who she is.

She enters Umalie's room and uses part of her bonus to replace the money she took from the piggy bank. She hangs the Mickey the Mouse umbrella from the side of her bed because Umalie always likes to have tools and toys at the ready when she wakes up. She leans forward to breathe in Umalie's smell. She rubs her nose against

Umalie's and kisses her head. Umalie stirs. She opens her eyes for a brief moment, and then rolls over onto her front, covering her head with her sheet.

Suspiciously Brown

'WHAT DO YOU do if you see a Paki with a broken leg?' Three-eyed Joe said down the phone.

Chief Preventive Officer Kevin Giblin of Her Majesty's Customs and Excise fiddled with his earpiece and stroked the three gold rings on the shoulder of his uniform as he waved a Caucasian family of four through the green channel at Heathrow Airport. 'Is this a joke?'

'Answer my question,' Three-eyed Joe said.

'I pull him in?'

'Correct, my friend. You pull him in.'

'What's he carrying?' Giblin asked. 'It better be worth my while this time.'

There was a pause. Then laughter. 'What's on every bleedin' news channel this side of the Great Wall of China?'

'The museum break-in?' Giblin asked.

'The man aims, he fires, he hits the goddamn target,'

Three-eyed Joe said. 'Yes, the museum robbery. Two stones from Sri Lanka. Heard of that place?'

'Beaches, tea, cricket. Of course I have.'

'The Blue Star of Lanka and the Star of Madras are sapphires,' Three-eyed Joe said.

'I thought you said they were both from Sri Lanka.'

'They are.'

Giblin sucked from a tube of toothpaste he kept in his pocket to hide the lingering smell of booze on his breath. 'But Madras is in India.'

'I'm no bloody gem merchant. Look the stones up.'

'You think I subscribe to *Sapphire Monthly*?'

'On the Internet, you twat. On the Internet. The point is, the three o'clock flight to Colombo tomorrow, look out for a Paki with a broken leg. The sapphires will be in his cast.'

'Hold on.' Giblin walked into an empty customs booth and shut the door. He took out a pen to take notes. 'Look mate, is this bona fide, legit intel? You know I'm on a warning for racism.'

'It's legit. Same source as always.'

'Your fence?' Giblin asked.

'No, my smuggler. The idea is not to sell these stones. The issue is repatriation. The stones were taken from Sri Lanka in colonial times. They asked for them back. Our boys said no, so word on the street is that a rich little Sri Lankan arranged for them to be taken.'

'So Sri Lankan, not Paki?'

'Same bloody thing.'

Back in his office, Giblin took a swig of vodka from a plastic water bottle and searched the Internet for the Blue Star of Lanka and the Star of Madras. They turned out to be the two most valuable sapphires in the world and of great historical relevance to Sri Lanka. The Star of Madras was named incorrectly which is one of the issues the government of Sri Lanka wanted rectified, repatriation being the other. Both requests were denied and rightly so, Giblin thought. Finders keepers and all that.

This could be just the high-profile catch Giblin needed. Maybe he would become known for a sapphire bust rather than for allegedly harassing Muslims. What if Three-eyed Joe was wrong, though? To be safe, Giblin considered passing this intel on to his superiors, but that would be like turning down the chance to take a penalty at a World Cup final, because you're thinking more about missing than scoring. With his career nose-diving as it was, he felt like he was drowning at sea and the only way into shore was on the back of a shark. If he did nothing he was going to drown anyway.

Giblin perched against a wall near the check-in counters for the relevant flight to Colombo. When he slouched, he noticed that part of his growing belly stuck out between the last two buttons of his shirt, but he did not allow this to distract him. Within moments he spotted a man with a broken leg, but with ginger hair and Tippex white skin – wasn't likely he'd be Sri Lankan. But the smaller details of intel are often wrong, Giblin thought. This had to be the man.

Giblin approached him and said, 'Can I help you, sir?'

The man looked at Giblin's uniform. 'No, can I help you?'

'Name, please.'

'Jason.' He held the crutches with his underarms and reached out a hand. 'Jason Jones.'

'Easy to remember.' Giblin noticed that Jason Jones did not look at all nervous or shifty. No one is this good. 'Would you mind just coming with me for a moment?'

Jason Jones smiled, a bit cockily. 'May I ask why?'

'When did you break your leg?'

'A couple months ago ... look, if you don't mind –' he pointed down at his cast '– I want to get to the departure gate so I can put my foot up.'

Giblin nudged Jason Jones to one side and looked over his right shoulder towards a brown man entering the terminal wearing a sleeveless puffer jacket that was four or five sizes too big, under which he had two sweaters, each frayed at the sleeves. His trousers were held up by a leather belt that looked like it had gone round his tiny waist twice. Most importantly he wore a leg cast that bulged in areas that were bright white and spotless.

Showtime.

Giblin didn't even bother speaking to Jason Jones again. He just brushed past him and marched up to the brown man the second he saw him queuing for the Colombo flight. 'Please come with me, sir,' he said.

The brown man was sweating so much he had to wipe his eyes. He leaned on his crutches, gave Giblin a half-hearted smile.

'Name?'

The brown man shrugged his shoulders. 'I'm sorry, what was that?'

'What's your name?'

The brown man smiled unsurely again. 'I'm struggling to pick up what you're saying,' he said in a nondescript accent. 'Are you from the north? I have always had trouble with northern dialects.'

'Look, sir,' Giblin said slowly, 'what is your name?'

'I am Mr Dias.'

'You need to come with me for a few moments.' Giblin spoke as slowly as he could, in an effort to mock this man who could not understand a Geordie accent. 'Just a routine check, sir.'

Giblin switched the clinical LED lighting on in the security office. He helped Mr Dias sit on a red chair, behind a spotless white table, facing two light-brown doors, with a long, thin window between them.

'May I?' Giblin said, lifting up Mr Dias's multi-coloured canvas shoulder bag. He looked up towards a camera in the corner of the room. 'I am not sure this gentleman understands what I am saying, but will proceed on the assumption that he does.'

He emptied the contents of the bag on the table. 'For the record we have one opened packet of Maliban

Lemon Puffs, a packet of chewing gum, loose change, and hello, sir, we have a number of pictures of scantily dressed ladies cut out of a magazine.' Giblin smiled at the camera and held up one of the pages. 'We also have a passport from the Democratic Socialist Republic of Sri Lanka.' He turned to the man. 'Sir, is this your passport?'

Mr Dias nodded.

Giblin turned the pages. 'Your name is Nimal Warnakulasuriya Patabendige Ushantha Dias. From the smirk on your face I am assuming that I have pronounced all those names just about as badly as is humanly possible.'

'You were close enough.' Dias looked at his watch. 'How long is this going to take? My flight leaves in less than two hours.'

Giblin smiled at the camera. 'With a bit of luck this will be over soon.' He flicked through the passport. 'You've been back and forth to countless countries around the world. Repeat visits.'

'It would appear so, yes.'

'What do you do?' Giblin asked.

'I travel.' He looked at his watch again. 'I have family around the world. Please, I'm really worried about missing my flight.'

'Be sure, sir, that if we find nothing on you I will personally escort you to your plane. Would you just allow me to search you? Like I said, it's strictly routine.'

'If you can be quick about it.'

Giblin looked up to the camera in the corner of the room and pulled on some disposable gloves. He slid his hands under Dias's armpits, pulling him to his feet. 'Are you okay to balance against the table?'

'Yes, sure,' Dias said.

Giblin felt up Dias's leg, his buttocks, around his groin, up his abs, under his belt, across his nipples. 'Sit, sit.' He picked up Dias's sandal and felt around the edges, knowing the shoe was too small to conceal sapphires but he had to check it all the same. He used his knuckles to knock against the entire length of each of Dias's crutches to make sure they were hollow.

'Now that you have searched me so intrusively, can I go?' Dias asked.

Giblin pointed at the cast. 'I am afraid I have not yet searched everything.'

'You're kidding me right?' Dias grabbed his crutches from against the wall. 'Please say you're kidding me.'

'Sir, I'm sorry.' Giblin reminded himself to speak slowly. 'I have to.'

'I asked my doctor about this before I booked my flight. As long as the cast has been on for over forty-eight hours, then it's okay to get on a plane.' Dias pulled something out of his wallet. 'This is a letter from him.'

'It's not about that.'

'Then if you're worried about explosives, I was told there was a swab test you could do. I have no problem with that.'

'I have reason to believe that you may have something hidden within your cast.' Giblin looked at the camera. 'His cast looks much bigger around the ankle and knee than it should be. The plastering also appears to be newer.'

'I am not sure I heard you right,' Dias said. 'But if you're worried about the knee and the ankle, yes it has been re-done because the plaster was softening.'

'I'm sure that's it,' Giblin said to the camera with a smile on his face. He pointed down at the cast and acted out scissors with his fingers. 'I am going to have to cut it off, I am afraid.'

'You will do no such thing.'

Giblin picked up the phone in the office when it rang.

'Superintendent Humphryes here. You can't cut the bloody cast off yourself.'

'Why not?' Giblin asked, cupping his hand around the phone. 'Clearly nothing wrong with his leg.'

'Is it plaster or fibreglass?"

'The cast?' Giblin asked.

'Yes, the bloody cast.'

'It's plaster.'

'I think you need a cast saw. Do you have a cast saw in your pocket?'

'I don't, sir, but you can also do this with shears.'

'Are you a doctor?'

'No, sir.'

'Then bloody wait for one.'

Moments later, after Giblin had helped himself to a cigarette break, Superintendent Humphryes arrived with a man who looked too young to be a doctor.

Humphryes shook Dias's hand. 'This doctor is going to have to use a cast saw on your leg, but I can promise you it will not cut you.'

'Wait a moment, here,' Dias said. 'There is no way in hell I am going to let you cut this off.'

'We can re-cast it for you afterwards,' Humphryes said.

The doctor plugged in the saw. Dias kicked his chair out from under himself and hobbled, on one leg, to the first of the two doors. 'Call me a lawyer, now.'

'Get back in the chair please, sir.' Giblin strode towards the door and pushed it shut. 'This won't take long.'

'Relax, sir,' Humphryes said. 'Relax.' He rolled his chair, on wheels, across to Dias. 'My name is Superintendent Humphryes. It is within my remit to make sure you are not hurt or unnecessarily inconvenienced.'

'You're about half an hour late,' Dias said.

'I am afraid you have no choice in the matter,' Humphryes said. He turned to Giblin. 'You're sure about this, right?'

Giblin nodded.

As they all guided Dias back to his chair he started screaming so high-pitched, the two customs officers and the doctor had to let go of him to cover their ears.

'You want me to sedate him?' the doctor asked.

'Don't you dare.' Dias pulled a chair towards himself and laboured into a seating position with his cast stretched out in front. He looked up at the ceiling and mouthed something to whichever god he assumed was looking out for him.

The doctor knelt down by the cast, holding it at the base and looking up as if plotting where to start. 'I need you to lie on your side on the table.'

'Your cooperation will be looked upon favourably,' Humphryes said.

Giblin placed a hand on the doctor's shoulder. 'Careful not to do any damage with that thing.'

The doctor shook his head. 'I think you'll find I know what I'm doing.' He crouched next to the cast, while Dias buried his head and began to chant something in his own language. He grimaced as the saw penetrated his cast.

'It won't hurt,' the doctor said. 'Just try to stay still.'

The saw made good progress but caught a snag at the knee. The doctor pulled it away. 'There could be something here.'

'Like some rocks?' Giblin smiled, rubbed his hands together, and slapped Humphryes on the back. 'Told you, sir.'

'No, no, no,' Dias said. He put both his hands around the top of his cast and pulled his leg away, but too late. The doctor had the cast loose and on the floor. He examined it closely, cutting it into thinner strips. 'My mistake. Nothing there but for poor plastering.' The doctor put the saw away.

'What the hell?' Giblin picked up the remains of the cast and started shaking it. 'Nothing?'

'Nothing' the doctor said. 'And his leg is clearly, very actually, definitely broken. Pretty badly. ' He pointed at Dias's shin. 'Right here.'

Dias grimaced as he moved his leg. 'I need a painkiller. It's astonishingly painful.'

'Yes,' the doctor said. 'Because it has not set yet, so now that I have removed the cast, the bones may not be kept in place.' He handed Dias a couple of ibuprofen tablets.

'I'm not going to make my flight, am I?' Dias asked.

No one answered.

Dias looked at the doctor. 'You wouldn't happen to have the time, would you?'

'Three forty-five.'

'There's another flight at seven-thirty. If I catch that I can still make my daughter's birthday.'

'Your daughter's birthday?' Humphryes asked.

'Four years old tomorrow. Can you get me on the flight?'

'What flight?' Humphryes asked, his eyes blank.

'Doctor,' Dias said, 'do you think you can recast my leg in time for me to catch the seven-thirty?'

'Not a chance, I'm afraid. We need to get you back to hospital. I need to see an X-ray before I can manipulate the bones into a cast. For now I'll have to splint it temporarily.' The doctor helped Dias to sit up on the table and got to work.

Dias took a deep breath. 'My wife is already on the verge of leaving me because I am never home for my family and now I am missing my daughter's birthday because that man over there –' he pointed at Giblin '– on a whim, thought I was hiding something in a cast for a leg that he thought was not actually broken, but very actually is. Is that a good summary of our situation?'

'Sir, rather than answering questions, let's see what we can do to get you home,' Humphryes said. 'There could be other flights.'

'There are no other flights,' Dias shouted. 'I checked. I checked because that is what grown men do when they have an important decision to make. Like how the doctor needs to check X-rays before he plasters my leg.' He pointed again at Giblin. 'That guy busted me based purely on the colour of my skin.'

'That's not true, sir,' Giblin said. 'I brought you in because you wore a leg cast.'

'So you're saying you picked me out of the crowd only because of my leg cast?'

'Yes –'

'So had you seen someone else with a leg cast, regardless of colour, you would have pulled him in instead – or at least, as well.'

'Yes, well ...' Giblin knew where he was going with this.

'Because when I first saw you, you were talking to another man with a cast.' Dias signalled for the doctor to be careful attaching the new splint. 'So I can safely assume he's next door, with his leg cast having been cut off. Doctor, did you cut off another man's leg cast?'

The doctor shook his head.

'I'm sorry,' Dias said, 'I don't understand all your English mannerisms. When you shake your head that means yes?'

'Means no,' the doctor said.

'That can't be,' Dias said. 'Because, just this second I was told that the matter of concern was a leg cast and that other man had one too.' Dias looked at Humphryes. 'You seem to be the boss here. Can I ask you, have you also brought in another man with a broken leg?'

'No, sir, but we had intel –'

'What's the difference between me and the other man with the broken leg?'

Silence.

'Well let me give you a clue.' He pointed at Giblin. 'What's your name?'

'Giblin, sir.'

'Well, Giblin, sir, what colour am I?'

'I'd rather not say.'

'Okay, I'll help you. I'm brown. Was the other man white?'

'The one with the broken leg?'

'Yes, the one with the broken leg?'

'Yes, he was white.'

'Did you let him go?'

'He wasn't acting suspiciously.'

'And I was?'

'Yes, you were, sir, I'm sorry.'

'So if I look up the word "suspicious", it will say anything brown?'

'It's not that,' Giblin said. 'You were sweating a lot, and you wouldn't give me your name when I first asked.'

'You're making an effort to speak slowly now,' Dias said. 'When you first approached me, with your accent, I didn't have a clue what you said.'

'It seems a bit convenient to blame it on my accent,' Giblin said.

'What exactly are you accusing me of?' Dias asked. 'Say it. Come on, I dare you.'

Humphryes held Giblin by the arm and pulled him away. 'Just leave it, okay?'

'No please,' Dias said. 'I want to hear more. What else does the colour of my skin and my inability to understand Northern dialects mean to you?'

'Nothing, sir,' Humphryes said.

'I want to hear it from him. You searched every nook and cranny of my being and found nothing, but still cannot accept you're wrong?' Dias slammed a hand on the table. 'So tell me, bad boy, what do you want to say?'

'Look, sir, maybe I made a mistake.'

'Oh that's big of you.'

'Clearly my intel was wrong.'

'Say it, big man, say it.'

'I'm sorry. It was a reliable source.'

'An informant?' Dias looked at Humphryes. 'Is that what you call them?'

'Yes, it is.'

'What did he tell you to look out for? A man in a cut-off puffer jacket and a cast?'

Giblin looked at the floor. 'He specifically said brown.'

Dias laughed again as if he couldn't help himself. 'But then why did you stop the whitest man in the world just because he had a broken leg? Are you colour-blind?'

'I wondered if the intel might have been wrong.'

'If it was wrong then why take in either of us?' Dias tapped the doctor on the shoulder. 'It hurts like hell. Can I have a cigarette please?'

Giblin shook his head. 'There's no smoking –'

'Just give him one,' Humphryes said.

Dias took his time lighting the cigarette. He pulled in long drags, frowning after each one. 'I am fundamentally lazy, and if I ever have a choice in life, I take the simplest route.' He looked down at his leg. The doctor had finished with the makeshift splint. 'If I could get on my crutches in time to catch another flight, I would just leave. Get to Sri Lanka and put this down to an awful, humiliating experience I want to put behind myself. But, you know what? Maybe it's a good thing I can't do that.'

'Sir,' Humphryes said, 'we'll do everything we can to patch you up so you're good to go for the next flight.'

'But I would have missed my daughter's birthday party already. Not to mention the shame of being taken in by customs officials in front of a bunch of Sri Lankan travellers. We are lovely people, but we're islanders and we gossip.'

'If there was anything I could do I would,' Humphryes said.

'There's a lot you can do.' Dias smiled, and stubbed out his cigarette. 'There's a lot you have to do if you don't want this to turn into a diplomatic incident.'

'What do you suggest?' Humphryes offered Dias another cigarette which he declined. 'I'm sure we can arrange for you to be taken straight to the very best hospital and we can put you up in the very best hotel until your flight leaves.'

Dias laughed. 'I'm not too enamoured of the idea of putting my health, accommodation or travel plans in your hands.'

'Then what?' Humphryes asked.

'I want justice and I'll stop at nothing short of it.' Dias clutched the sides of his chair as if to help himself up. 'I'm disinclined to accept anything from you, because that will look like compensation. I don't want compensation. Just get me a wheelchair and put me in a taxi.'

'To take you to hospital?' Humphryes asked.

'No, to take me to my lawyers.'

The next day Giblin woke up naked and alone on the sofa. He couldn't remember anything from the purposefully mind-numbing pub crawl he found himself on the night before. The doorbell rang. Giblin covered himself with cushions and had a peak through the letterbox. Humphryes stood outside, tapping his feet fast and tearing bits of paper off the corner of a brown envelope.

Giblin said. 'Sir, it's my day off.'

'Dias has calmed down.' Humphryes leaned against the door. 'Please just let me in.'

'Give me a minute.' Giblin found the previous night's clothes strewn across the living room floor. He smelled the shirt and it was all smoke and vomit so he chucked that behind the sofa, and put on the trousers.

Giblin lit a cigarette, opened the door and sat down on the sofa with his head in his hands. 'Please tell me this is good news.'

'He wants ten thousand pounds, a business-class ticket to Sri Lanka, a limousine to pick him up from his hotel, and an airport buggy to take him from the limo, through immigration, all the way to the plane.'

'Ten thousand pounds?'

'We may be able to get him to come down on that. His main issue is he doesn't want to be pulled in again for being, as he said, suspiciously brown.'

'The guy's bloody fishy,' Giblin said. 'I'm telling you.'

'I wouldn't risk your career over that,' said Humphryes. 'Besides, he had one other request.'

Giblin laughed. 'He wants me to help him clear security?'

'And drive him all the way to the plane,' Humphryes said. 'Is that something you can do?'

'I have no choice, right?'

Dias sat on the flight to Colombo next to Sidhara Beckham, a short Sri Lankan man with a cockney accent. Dias knew he should keep a low profile, but once introduced he was intrigued to find out how this man had such a South Asian first name, but an English surname.

It turned out that a family based in London had adopted Sidhara from Buddhist monks twenty-nine years earlier. 'Then last month,' he said, 'I was contacted by a man who calls himself Leg-Breaker Gunesekera; do you know of him?'

'Who doesn't,' Dias said. 'Have you seen *Pulp Fiction*?'

Sidhara nodded.

'Well, you know the character Harvey Keitel plays?'

'Mr Wolf?'

'Leg-Breaker Gunesekera is the Sri Lankan equivalent. He can fix anything. So he found you?'

'Yes and put me in touch with a guy who put me in touch with my mother, with one proviso. I could never tell her that they found me. I had to say that I found her.'

'And so here you are. Your first time to the motherland?' Dias asked.

'First time in Asia.'

'I think you will feel you belong,' Dias said.

'I don't know,' Sidhara said. 'I hope so.'

Dias looked down at his leg cast. 'Everything that leaves Sri Lanka, always comes back.'

Sidhara pushed Dias, in his wheelchair, through the airport. When they cleared customs and entered the arrival lounge, Dias saw a lady in her late forties, with chiselled arms and noticeably defined cheekbones, dressed as if she was going to the Oscars.

'Sidhara?' She dropped to her knees. 'Oh praise the lord, Sidhara.' She looked to the ceiling. 'My God is so encompassing and ever present. My prophet is so powerful. Come to me, son. Come to me.'

'I'll be fine,' Dias said. 'Go to her.'

Sidhara's mother got back on her feet, and clutched on to him with all her strength. 'My little baby boy. My little baby boy.'

Despite knowing that he should get out of the airport as soon as possible, Dias stayed and watched. Sidhara buried his face in the gap between his mother's shoulder and neck and closed his eyes. Rather awkwardly, at that very moment, his mother seemed to break wind.

Dias whispered, 'Goodbye,' but before he could wheel himself over to tap Sidhara on the back, he felt someone pull at his arm. A customs official got behind his wheelchair and pushed it back through the swing doors and into a brightly lit office. A Caucasian man with ginger hair stood in the corner, speaking on the phone. At first, Dias did not recognize him without his leg cast.

The man put out his hand. 'Good morning, Mr Dias. My name is Jason Jones. I have a close friend of Madam President on the phone and he has one very important question to ask. Did it work?'

'Yes,' Dias said, pointing at his leg cast. 'I have the stones.'

Graveyard Tail

JANITH LAKMAL STRAPS Kayaan, his nine-month-old baby, in the back of his silver Audi but his three-year-old daughter, Umalie, is still in her room insisting on putting on her own clothes. Ideally Janith would ask the maid to watch Kayaan, but that is not possible because he asked her to leave ten days ago. So he unstraps him, and by the time he gets to Umalie she has both her legs in the same pipe of her trousers (which she calls 'pants' because, much to his chagrin, Janith's wife was educated in the States). Now, for the first time ever in her long and illustrious career as a pre-schooler, Umalie wants to tidy up her toys. Janith bribes and threatens her – Pablo Escobar's silver-or-lead approach – and she is in the car but she refuses to get in her seat because she wants to put her baby brother to sleep – the same baby brother who had fallen asleep in his father's arms before Umalie woke him up so that she could get him to sleep. Then she wants to get out of the car to stroke Eddie, the family's adopted street dog. 'Can Eddie sleep in my room tonight?'

Janith is about to snap. He needs to get the kids to and from the doctor so he can get back to trying to secure the Port City contract. Failing to do so is not an option, now that the family life savings (including the unofficial dowry he got from his wife's father) is tied up in a fund managed by a man who has been convicted of fraud. To ensure he will win the contract, he has hired Leg-Breaker Gunesekera, a private investigator, to spy on his rival bidder. He has to be ready to strike as soon as he learns of the figures. This time-wasting is not appreciated.

Since the maid left, every day Janith has had to bathe one or other of the kids, put them to bed, and generally allocate more hours to them than he can afford. His wife has also chosen this of all times to let him know she wants another child, and Janith cannot tell her that he can barely afford to feed and clothe the two kids they have already. The only time Janith can be alone is late at night and now he barely sleeps. He rubs his temples and takes a deep breath. 'But look how dirty his paws are.'

'Then can we give him a bath before we go?' Umalie opens the door and tries to get out.

'Sit down and shut that door right now.' Janith surprises himself with how loud he shouts. Kayaan wakes and starts crying, while Umalie looks stunned, before she too breaks down in tears.

'I'll never let you have Eddie in your room unless you stop crying.'

'You hurt my ears, Daddy,' Umalie says. 'With your shouting, you hurt my ears.'

Janith punches the steering wheel three times. 'I'm sorry, okay, but please stop crying. Please, I can't take it.' He thinks about getting out of the car and running down the street to buy some cigarettes even though he quit eighteen months ago. 'Where is your mother?'

Umalie is crying too much to be able to answer, so Janith gets out of the Audi and slams the door. He looks back and can see the kids crying but he cannot hear them.

They have sixteen minutes to get to the doctors. He knows he is up against it because his wife's appearance is significantly more important to her than being on time for a highly qualified, but socially inept medical practitioner. He runs up the stairs to drag his wife down them.

They are in the car.

Now they are out of the garage but Umalie says she has forgotten her Mickey the Mouse umbrella.

'It's not raining,' Janith says.

They go back to get the umbrella, and sure enough, it begins to rain. Umalie smiles.

They seem to be going in the right direction finally, crossing the paddy field, and driving up the steep slope of the former rubber estate they live on and onto Hokandara Road. As they turn right onto Kanatte Road, their car is almost hit by a green tuktuk, and then a second later by a large red jeep with VIP licence plates. Janith hears a police siren and notices a woman on a Batman-like motorbike, coming in their direction before hitting the green tuktuk, knocking it on its side. The woman loses control of her bike and slides towards the red VIP jeep, which in swerving to avoid her, runs over a black-and-brown dog.

The bike and the lady on it skid past Janith's Audi, smacking into the bare cement brick wall of an abandoned house.

'Jesus,' Janith says, as his car comes to a stop. He takes off his seatbelt and turns around to cover Umalie's eyes. 'Put your head between your knees and wait there.'

Umalie is too stunned to react. Janith gets out of the car and runs back to where the motorbike came to rest. The woman is trapped under it. She is wearing a helmet that looks like it belongs in a World War II movie, and there is blood pouring out of the bottom of her skull. By sliding across the asphalt, her clothes have been shredded. Janith notices that she has a devil mask tattoo just above her exposed breasts. He looks up the road and sees a man getting out of the red jeep, bending down as if to check on the tuktuk driver. A muscular lady in a drenched fluorescent yellow tank top stands next to the dead dog screaming, 'Stop that man, stop that man.' The man limps back to his red jeep and speeds off, but not before Janith has used his phone to take a photo of the licence plate.

A police car stops right next to the lady on the motorbike.

When Janith gets back to the car, he thinks he will have to placate his kids but it is actually his wife who is howling. He is not surprised that the cause of her anguish is the dead dog. When they first met, she dived (she would say 'dove') out of a moving car when Janith would not stop to help a wounded cat.

The dog is ten metres ahead of his car, on its front, covered in blood, its legs mangled, its tongue hanging out. The lady who previously shouted out at the man in the red jeep sits by the dog's side, stroking its head. She must be in her late forties, and has a defined jaw, but thinning hair.

Janith gets back into the car, putting it in gear, before his wife grabs his wrist.

'We have to help her,' she says.

Janith disagrees. This is not his responsibility. The Port City contract is. His kids are. He points back at them and says, 'We're leaving. Otherwise we're going to get tied up in this as witnesses.'

'Please.' His wife's hands are up in prayer. 'We have to.'

The muscular lady looks up at Janith and points to the dog. Now that she has seen him, he can't drive off. 'Okay, I'll see what I can do.' Janith opens the door and looks at his wife. 'Get the kids to the doctor and when I get home, you really can't disturb me or I –'

'Yes, I know. Port City.'

Janith grabs a towel from Kayaan's baby bag and slams the door. He signals for his wife to drive off, before he remembers that he didn't say bye to his crying kids. He strolls up to the lady on the road, placing the towel on her shoulders because she is dripping with water even though the rain has stopped.

'Save him,' she screams. 'Save him.'

Bending down, Janith pretends to feel for a heartbeat but the dog could not be more dead. His eyes are wide open. 'I'm sorry, madam, I think –'

'Don't say he's dead,' she says, her face nestled in Janith's shoulder. 'Aiyo cannot die. He's a survivor.' She holds him and does not let go. 'He never dies.'

Police cars and ambulances gather twenty metres down the road where the lady on the Batman bike is lying dead. Hardly anyone is paying attention to the apparent corpse under the tuktuk.

Janith sits next to the lady in silence for over ten minutes, when she seems to change her tune. She turns to Janith. 'I need to bury him in the cemetery.'

Looking around, Janith realizes he could not help even if he wanted to. The cemetery is overcrowded and messy, with gravestones literally on top of each other. 'I don't think we can,' he says. 'There are no free plots.'

'There are two.' She points to the far corner of the cemetery, under a jack tree. 'I know because I bought them.'

It is forty minutes later and there is mayhem down the road. Janith and the lady have already been interviewed by the police and they find out that the biker lady was a suspect in the Sky City killings. There are news crews, including the BBC, plus six army jeeps and countless policemen.

Janith has blood all over his white linen shirt. He has carried the dead dog, covered in a blue plastic sheet he found lying around, to the spare plots the lady mentioned, and now he is lifting up a shovel axe. 'Are you sure this plot is empty?'

The lady nods. 'Don't worry, you're not going to find bones there.'

Texting his wife to say he will be late, Janith wonders what the hell he has got himself into here. He hands the lady his phone. 'If I'm digging, you may need to answer this.'

'I can do that.' The lady seems incredibly calm now. She is curling her hair around her right index finger. She stops, looks at her finger, and then combs her hair back into place to cover areas on her head which are close to being bald. She holds her right hand down with her left, as if stopping it from doing further damage to her hair. 'I saw you take a photo of the red jeep,' she says.

Janith has just started digging and doesn't want to lose momentum so he nods his head.

'I screamed at the man, but I don't know if it was his fault. I guess he either had to run over Aiyo or run over that lady. I hope one day I find him so I can look him in the eye and ask him why he didn't come to me to say sorry.'

Shaded a little by the jack tree, the humidity is high and the earth is hard, so Janith has his work cut out and the last thing he needs is a conversation with this lady. He just hopes he will hear the phone if it rings. He notices the grave next to where he is digging is in immaculate condition. 'You are sure this plot is free?'

'Unless I have been sold a used one,' she says.

'Your plot is definitely this one, right?' Janith stops digging. 'I mean if it isn't and I dig up someone's body, I'm going to jail. I'm just not sure –'

'You look tired, and I have no water to give you.' She taps the mud next to where she sits. 'Come, sit for a few minutes.' The lady has already pulled a photo album out of her bag. 'Please.'

Janith's phone rings and the lady hands it to him. It is not Leg-Breaker Gunesekera, so Janith turns the sound off and puts it in his pocket. He sits down next to the lady.

'If I were you,' she says, 'with all these cops around, and with a mad lady asking you to dig a hole in a graveyard, I would have run a mile.'

'I thought about it,' Janith says. 'But you look like you're dressed to chase me.'

The lady smiles and opens the photo album. On the first page there is a photograph of a chubby adolescent wearing thick glasses. She points to the grave.

'Oh, I'm so sorry,' Janith says. 'A loved one?'

'No, no.' She turns the page to another couple of photographs of him. 'Not really. I mean, yes. Ashan was one of my students.'

Janith looks at the dates on the gravestone. 'Too young.' He wants to know how he died, but knows he should not ask.

The lady turns another page. Now there is a photo of the boy lying on the brown-and-black dog, almost using him as a pillow. 'Ashan had Asperger's Syndrome. It means he didn't really relate to anyone. But Aiyo got something out of him. I thought Aiyo was going to be special. The lady bows her head and wipes her eyes. I thought he was going to be ...' She allows the album to drop off her lap.

Janith picks the album up from the mud and turns the page to a photograph of Aiyo alone. He looks like just about every other brown-and-black stray dog in the country. Kind of like a Doberman runt. Janith keeps turning the pages past more and more pictures of Aiyo and Ashan, until right at the end of the album where there is a sole faded photograph of a bald baby boy. He looks a little too dark and the photograph a little too old for it to be Ashan, but it could be.

'Ashan's parents were ashamed of him,' the lady says. 'Too ashamed to let him have a normal life. Too ashamed to even give him a funeral.' She snatches the album back from Janith. 'Our people worry too much about what the neighbours think. But, you know, they really loved him. I know they did. So I bought two graves next to Ashan in case they wanted to be with him. I mean, they won't know what I know. They won't know how much it means.'

'To be buried together?' Janith asks.

'Just to be together.' She turns to the last page of the album. 'Sidhara.' She strokes the plastic sleeve above the photograph.

In the silence that follows, Janith slaps away the flies collecting around Aiyo's body and then watches down the road as the dead body under the tuktuk is wrapped in a sheet and flung, rather unceremoniously, into the back of an ambulance. Janith feels queasy, like blood is collecting up his nose and at the back of his mouth. Like blood is rushing to his head. And all around him, blood. He checks his phone and still no news from Leg-Breaker.

'Are you Sri Lankan?' the lady asks.

'One hundred per cent Sinhala Buddhist,' Janith says.

'You don't have to be Sinhalese to be Sri Lankan.'

'But you have to be Sri Lankan to be Sinhalese,' he says, without knowing what he means. 'Why do you ask?'

The lady smiles. 'It's just that, Sri Lankans normally ask more personal questions, like ...'

'Like who is the baby?'

'Exactly.'

'And if I were to ask that?'

'I'd tell you simply that he is my son who I have not seen since he was two months old. I'd tell you that

I always thought he'd find me, and that I have been waiting twenty-nine years. I'd tell you, I will never give up waiting.'

'And if I asked you if you have tried to find him?'

'I would nod. I would tell you to mind your own business, but only because I am afraid to give you my answer.'

'But if you weren't what would you say?'

'My, you are a Sri Lankan after all.' She smiles. 'I would say that I tracked him down to Wandsworth in London, where he was brought up by Mr and Mrs Beckham. I'd tell you I was too scared to contact him because maybe he wouldn't want to hear from me. I'd tell you I didn't want to mess up his life. I'd tell you he needs to find me.'

'He will, I am sure.'

'He's certainly taking his time, but the future is in God's hands now. As my darling Aiyo will be, if you ever get around to burying him.'

Janith gets home past midnight and uses the garden tap to wash the soil off his hands and shoes. A layer of skin has come off his thumb and he has splinters on his left palm from the shovel axe handle. He takes Eddie to the tap and washes his paws, then leads him up to Umalie's room and onto her bed. He kisses them both and goes next door where he puts his hand on Kayaan's chest to make sure he is breathing. He tiptoes into the master bedroom and lies down next to his sleeping wife. He looks at the thirty-three missed calls from Leg-Breaker Gunesekera on his phone and checks his text messages. One says, 'I've emailed you the figures.'

Janith replies with an attached photo of the red jeep: 'I'll look at the figures in a few minutes. Please get me contact details for the person who owns this jeep. Also, this may sound odd, but I need to find a twenty-nine-year-old man living in Wandsworth.'

Balls

MANJULA IS NOT the reason I am gay, of course he isn't, but I need him to be here when I come out. We grew up together; in middle school our cricket made us equally high-profile, but then he blossomed into the kind of boy no one could keep their eyes off. Even mothers coming to pick up their kids would whisper about his looks in a way that would be creepy if it was fathers talking about young girls. Uncommonly for a Sri Lankan, he has green eyes; always did to be honest, but when we were younger they made him look a little scary and intense against his dark skin. Now they make him smoulder.

For much of our adolescent lives, we competed for the same things, be it on the cricket pitch, in the classroom or around the canteen where the girls hung out. Yet, whereas my talents stagnated after puberty, Manjula's exploded.

I owe him massively on two counts. Firstly, before I came to terms with my sexuality, we went head to head over the same girl and he backed down. This was partly noble, but partly arrogant because he knew he had a greater selection of suitors to choose from. Secondly, he knew I dreamed of getting into Harvard so he did not apply there himself. The top universities in the US usually accept just one Sri Lankan student a year, if that, and sure enough Manjula got into every place to which he'd applied, even though I cannot understand why he even considered America when it is so obvious he is going to play international cricket.

I didn't get Harvard, but it's the thought that counts.

The only time I have argued with Manjula is over religion. Like my mother, he is a devotee of Prophet Conrad Cecil who is either deluded or just a conman, I can't tell. Either way he preys on those in strife. My mother was an obvious target as she has had a tough life. As much as I try to pretend that he didn't, my father beat her regularly when he drank before she was finally able to banish him. Since then there have been two other people in my life I called Thathi, but neither of them seemed noble in their intentions towards her. But Manjula? Sure his parents don't come to watch him play cricket or sing at carol services, but he has them both. And he's the most talented, hardworking person in the world, so it bugs the hell out of me when he says his success is thanks to Prophet Conrad Cecil and the Lord (in that order). I tell him he deserves the credit himself, but he just crosses himself and rolls his eyes, confident that he will be able to convert me one day.

Manjula is a quarter Brazilian, a quarter Tamil and half Sinhalese but will not admit to anything beyond being Sri Lankan. He's the best cricketer his age in the country as well as being the best footballer, the best swimmer, the best athlete, the best debater, the best actor, and the best damn singer in our school. This makes him confident, which is good for me because when I come out he won't need to pretend to be homophobic in case anyone thinks he is gay himself.

I am pretty sure the others in the car will do that.

Manjula and I are sitting in the back of a Honda Civic. The sunroof is open. Prince's 'Alphabet Street' is thumping out beats through the surround-sound stereo system.

Ramesh is driving. He claims to be eighteen, so our age, but he's balding, has aggressive stubble and talks about politics and the stock market. When not with us, his school friends, he hangs out at the 100 Club with CEOs of major local companies, politicians and other alcoholics.

Next to him in the front is Rajiv. He is also balding because he uses too many chemicals to spike his hair, but it doesn't hide from the fact that he has one of the ugliest noses I have ever seen. It spans pretty much his whole face, from ear to ear, and looks like three tennis balls squashed together.

Ramesh is essentially an old man in a young man's body. Actually it's a fairly old man's body. Young man's clothes, let's say, since he is in the dark and light beige combo that is a Sri Lanka International School uniform. So I'm not sure what to expect from him when I come out – maturity, but maybe also an old-fashioned belief that homosexuality is immoral. Still, I expect a more asinine reaction from Rajiv which will likely border on blind homophobia to cover up the fact that he himself has had homosexual urges. I know he has, because he is always the ring-leader for the homo-erotic birthday surprises my group of friends spring on each other. They sometimes involve a razor and they always involve stripping.

Being honest with my friends is a big damn deal, not just for me, but I think for anyone else in the school system in Sri Lanka who wants to come out. I've cleared the biggest hurdle in telling my mum already. She shines a light on how liberal she is all the time, so she was always going to hug me, say it changes nothing and then try to fix me up with a man before realizing that's really, really weird.

My father is busy being a sober daddy to a new family of heterosexuals so I doubt it would even register with him – maybe as the rugger bugger he is, it may embarrass him but that can only be a good thing.

Now it's just my friends I have to tell. The same friends I have been cracking gay jokes with since I was thirteen. The same friends who I competed with for girls. The same friends I have shared beds with, ragged, changed with. The same friends who will think I am the last person, other than Manjula, who could ever be gay.

Hell, until two weeks ago, I was dating Ishara, the female equivalent of Manjula – in looks at least. She has polled Best-looking Girl in school every July since Grade 7. Her legs are just out of this world, all muscle and smoothness and I am not sure how the school lets her get away with the minimalistic cut of her red P.E. shorts. When I knew I was being unfair to her, and possibly to Manjula, we broke up. She threatened to end the relationship first, but when I said *you betcha* she said, *say what*? She got down on those special knees of hers and begged. Rolled out the whole hair-pulling, make-up-running antics I thought were beneath her. Said she's never been so hurt in her life, but you know what? She never liked me anyway. It was always Manjula this, Manjula that, photo with Manjula, fluttering eyelids, the works.

I wonder how she will take the news when she hears I am gay. Maybe relief that that's why I moved on from her, or maybe fear that people will joke that she made me gay.

As if circumstance makes people gay.

I'm not kidding myself. I know some of the older parents – those who went to single-sex schools and who experimented with their batchmates but think that's not being gay – will ban their kids from seeing me in case my homosexuality is infectious. But this is two thousand

and goddamn ten. Everything I stand for is wrong if I do not have the balls to be myself.

So it is the moment. I'm about to do it.

'Guys, I have something to tell you.'

'What's that?' asks Rajiv.

'Nothing. Hahaha.'

Manjula's hand's on my thigh. He may regret that. 'Come on, you got something on your chest?'

I say, 'I'm gay.'

'Hahahaha. No, come on, dude, really. You brooding over Ishara?'

'Ishara? You're kidding me, machang? I'm telling you I'm gay.'

Rajiv laughs. 'You like penis, I show you mine.'

'Guys. I. Am. Gay. Really, I am. Please, listen, I want to come out and I want my friends to take this seriously.'

'You swear on your life?' Ramesh asks.

'Swear on my life.'

The car screeches to a stop, the steering wheel going crazy in Ramesh's hand.

Rajiv jumps out the car first and pretends to hurl into the drain because he thinks that's what he has to do to show he's straight.

Ramesh is out next. Cracking up. 'You share his bed all the time,' he says to Rajiv. 'Lights out, he likely cops a feel.'

'Come on, guys,' says Manjula. 'Shut up.'

'Thanks machang, means a lot,' I say.

'He's not really gay.' Manjula says.

'Dude, what have I got to do to prove it to you?'

Manjula's out the back of the car before I can say paint me pink. He's on the sidewalk, wanting to do the right thing. Thinking, thinking but worried. Everyone he has ever met who likes boys likes him. Would that include me?

'Oh come on, Manjula, I'm not going to hit on you.'

He puts up his hand to stop me talking. 'Course you're not,' he says. Clearly he doesn't believe it. He's a modest guy for all he has, but the dude thinks everyone wants him. School girls, teachers and gays.

The news is on Twitter before I get home and the one picture of me in a pink shirt is circulated around all social media platforms.

Ishara tweets: 'That explains everything. #GAYPASINDU'

Rajiv tweets: 'I didn't know when I slept in his bed. #GAYPASINDU'

Manjula tweets: 'Cut him some slack, guys. He's still the Pasindu we all love. #GAYPASINDU'

Rajiv tweets: 'Manjula loves #GAYPASINDU lolololololol'

This is all mind-numbingly childish stuff so I switch off my computer, a hand-me-down from Manjula, and close my eyes for hours.

All the gay jokes hurt me, sure they do, but not as much as I expected. I know I'm today's news, but soon these cats will have other scraps to fight over. I skip a couple of days from school all the same and, just in case the news has spread, I avoid the gym too. I text my trainer, Chin-up Channa, but there is no reply, which is extremely unusual – perhaps he too has cut me off for being gay.

I get a visit from Mr Dilano, the Physics teacher with the English accent who thinks he has convinced everyone he is straight. His heart's in the right place, I know, *but shit, Ammi, why'd you open the door to him? I told you I wanted to be alone.*

'Someone I know went through this themselves,' Mr Dilano says. 'You're not alone.'

I want to say, *I wish I was.*

'You know, you're a hero really,' he says. 'I am sure this person I know wished he was just like you. Not hiding all the time.'

'Thanks, sir.'

'I mean it,' he says.

'I know, sir.'

'Can I hug you?'

Three bags full, sir.

We hug, which is odd considering this is my secretly gay teacher and this is my openly gay bedroom. Mr Dilano leaves with a smile and tears.

So I think that's a wrap, but there is another knock at my bedroom door. 'I've got a real special guest for you, son,' my mum says. 'Prophet Conrad Cecil.'

In walks the American with a bulbous nose and thinning blond hair. I've met him before but have never acknowledged him nor him me. Ishara told me it was because I looked too confident for him to be able to win me over, but then what happened to Manjula?

Prophet Conrad Cecil ambles around my room and is all *Praise the Lord* and *God be Praised*. He's all arms in the air and eyes rolled back and he tells me he's proud of me for coming out. He tells me God told him he was cool with it. Very cool. As long as I am fearful of him. Of his anger if I screw up.

'What does screwing up mean?' I ask.

'You know, messing with kids,' he says.

'You do know gays are not paedophiles, right?'

'Some are,' he says.

'So are some priests and prophets.'

'Touché,' he says. 'Look, I'm speaking to the big guy about you and he's a fan.'

'A fan?' I laugh.

'He wants to shine down praise and faith on you, but only if you worship at his big feet.'

'Are you for real?'

'Hold my hands and pray with me and I will forever be on your side.'

My mother looks in on us, so I hold the fruitcake's hand and close my eyes. I can't bring myself to repeat his drivel.

He seems pleased with himself. Standing, he closes his eyes and looks up.

'Make a contribution,' my mother says.

Prophet Conrad Cecil has a bag open.

I laugh because this is a man who has so much money he didn't mind losing four million dollars on Chinthika Balasuriya's Ponzi scheme. 'You want my pocket money?'

He points up. 'Not me, son. Not me. You'll feel the big guy's embrace.'

That's the gayest thing I've heard since I came out.

I'm back at school and have to contend with two opposite camps of people.

Camp 1: Those going out of their way to pretend they're cool with me being gay, but they trip up and say things like 'Make yourself at homo' when I go to their houses.

Camp 2: Led by my old pal Rajiv, and other friends who have shared clothes, beds and jacuzzis with me. They go out of their way to show how disgusting they find me.

Manjula's the most normal in my presence, but when the homosexual homophobes start telling him that I said I wanted to sleep with him, I hear from him less regularly. I don't think he means anything by this. He genuinely believes that he's so desirable that people can't resist him. Hell, you can't blame him. Our so-called conservative female classmates throw themselves at him all the time, and he ends up distancing them in the same way he is me.

I understand this and I'm not bitter, but I would have liked him to hold my hand through this, figuratively speaking.

Today, during lunch break, I see a semicircle of admirers gathered around Manjula laughing at his jokes. They don't notice me coming towards them.

Manjula says, 'Pasindu's life without women will be a pain in the ass.'

Everyone in the crowd cracks up, but Manjula holds up his hand and says, 'Wait, I have more. What do Pasindu and Tom Cruise have in common?'

Hush.

'They have both been in a *Few Good Men.*'

The laughter breaks out and doesn't stop. I think Manjula sees me but I run off before we have to have an astonishingly awkward conversation. I've heard all these jokes before, but just not from Manjula. Maybe I would have done the same if I was straight and he came out, but I doubt it.

I feel very alone, but I don't cry. All this feels surreal, because I am floating in and out of these conversations without any desire to react. In some ways it is a relief that Manjula has joined the others in making fun of me. I feel like I have let him down. We were the girl-chasing double act and now it is just him. Yet, he has chosen his path. He has chosen to mock me so let him live his life and I will live mine, with no responsibility to anyone but myself.

It's time for the Graduation Ball, so I am hopeful people will tweet less about me. The big topic is: who is Manjula going to ask to be his date?

‘I heard he’s taking GayPasindu’s ex. #Ball’

‘Manjula asked Pasindu’s ex Ishara to the ball. #Ball’

‘GayPasindu’s really pissed off. #Ball’

And so it goes on and on and Manjula does nothing to quell the rumours. He tweets:

‘Plucking up the courage to ask the most beautiful person in the world to the #Ball #ManjulaDate’

I thought I was in the clear, but there is the odd tweet directly about me too.

‘Who’ll Pasindu take? #Ball’

‘Maybe Pasindu will take Mr Dilano. #Balls’

Retweeted 47 times.

‘Like oh my God, dudes, how funny,’ I reply when I should have remained silent.

I’m not going to the ball anyway, but still all I hear is that Manjula has been looking for me. They say he wants to ask me for permission to take Ishara. I feel nothing for her, so I have no idea why it pisses me off so much that he is even thinking about asking her. My mother says he has called the landline sixteen times.

I’m not going to the ball for two reasons; one, I don’t want to see anyone and two, for school balls you have to have a date, but who the hell would go with me?

The bell rings and Ammi tells me I have a special visitor again. Oh man, this is no time for a prophet to profit from my predicament. I just want to be normal.

I run down the stairs, ready to sprint past Conrad Cecil, but it’s not him and it’s not Mr Dilano either.

It’s Manjula.

'What the heck you doing here?' I ask.

'Who were you expecting?' he asks. 'God?'

'Pretty close. Prophet Conrad Cecil, in fact.'

'Didn't you hear?' Manjula crosses himself. 'They've arrested him.'

'Say what?'

'I can't believe you don't know.' Manjula raises his arms. 'Have you locked yourself in a closet for the last week?'

I look at my feet and shake my head.

'Oh yeah, sorry.' Manjula says. 'Chin-up Channa was arrested for stalking that yummy mummy we fancied … well, the yummy mummy I fancied. To save his own skin, the pig-faced bastard ratted on the great prophet. The man who saved his life.'

'Chin-up Channa? Wow. I guess it's always the silent ones.'

'Conrad Cecil's clearly innocent,' Manjula says. 'Don't forget, Jesus was persecuted too.'

'Oh by God!' I say.

'No, by the Romans and Jews, but that's for another time. What's important is that you know I'm not gay.'

'Yes,' I say, 'I do appreciate not everyone who comes to my door has to be.'

'But honestly, please acknowledge that you know I'm not.'

I nod. Place my hand on my heart. 'I know,' I say. 'I promise.'

Manjula steps back, away from the front door. He says, 'Can you come out please?'

I say, 'I already have.'

'No, I mean step outside your house.'

'I know. I know. You homophobes don't have a monopoly on gay jokes.'

He beckons me over towards the jack tree at the far end of the garden. He brushes dirt off the bench before inviting me to sit down, but keeps enough distance to show he still thinks I may pounce on him.

'Okay, Pasindu, I feel guilty,' he says, facing away from me. I can just see the side of his face.

'You needn't –'

'Please just let me finish. Not been sleeping well. I've imagined how tough things must be for you, and I know if I was in your position I'd never have had the guts to be honest about it. Yet, when you told us, I didn't really stand up for you. Didn't hug you and say, you know what, you're still one of my best friends. Of all time.

'And when people made fun of you behind your back, I didn't stop them. Didn't say a thing, even though I'm the main ... you know, I don't want to sound arrogant –'

'– you're the main man in school,' I say. 'Honest truth.'

'And yeah, so often what I say goes.'

'Always does,' I say.

'So my silence made it look like I thought it was okay for those knobs to make fun of you because they're insecure.'

'I heard your jokes too, dude.'

'I thought you did,' he says. 'I feel awful, but it wasn't how I feel. I mean, I just wanted some laughs.'

'At my expense,' I say.

'I know, and you're like a brother to me. How could I do that to you?'

'Don't knock yourself over this, machang,' I say.

'Word on the street is that you're not coming to the ball,' he says.

'The street's right,' I say.

'Machang, this is our last one. Our graduation. The end of our youth. You have to come.'

'Everyone has to have a date,' I say.

Manjula clasps his hands together and closes his eyes. 'I've come here to ask you something.'

Here it comes. All this crap just so he can ask me if he can take Ishara to the ball. When we were younger we used to fight a lot. Like brothers, really. When Manjula really pissed me off I used to wrestle him to the ground knowing I was stronger than him. Yet, somehow he would always end up on top of me, with my arms pinned. I wonder if I am too old now to wrestle him to the grass when he finally asks me if he can disrespect me by taking my ex-girlfriend to the ball when I don't have a date.

'The ball is huge,' Manjula says.

'And I love huge balls, right?'

Manjula laughs. 'Seriously, bro, this is so big. I wouldn't normally ask this as it's very, very awkward, but it's important that I take someone to the ball I really like. Really admire. I could just take anyone but it wouldn't mean the same.'

I nod. *Spit it out, man. Spit it out. You think you're such a tough guy. You think everyone will think you're so noble for asking me, to my face, about dating my ex-bird but you know what's more noble? Not taking her.*

'And you know,' he says, 'everyone's so caught up in who I'm going to take.'

'Everyone, machang,' I say. 'Including me.'

'So I can send a message,' he says. 'I can make a statement about what I think it means to grow up.'

'By whom you take to the ball?' I ask.

Manjula turns to face me directly. Puts his hands on my shoulders. 'Everyone needs a date to get into the Graduation Ball.'

'So I have been told a million times,' I say.

Manjula holds his hands up in prayer. 'I would be deeply honoured, Pasindu Amarasinghe, if you would come to the ball as my date.'

Acknowledgements

KANISHKA GUPTA, SUPER-AGENT and all-round nice guy for supporting his authors far beyond the call of duty.

Pia Hatch, Sri Lanka's most selfless and brilliant PR guru – should you be sick of seeing me in too many magazines and newspapers, you can blame her.

Neelini Sarkar, the first person who ever sees my writing. I would never have been published without her suggestions and encouragement.

The editors of my previous books for showing me the way: the debonair Amish Mulmi and the incredible Manasi Subramaniam.

Diya Kar Hazra – for my manuscript to be acquired by someone so well-known and respected was such a great honour. I am grateful to her for challenging me to be better, to work harder and to make this as good as my limited talent will allow.

The delightful Teesta Guha Sarkar for editing this book with so much professionalism, flair and kindness. In my long and questionable career as a human being, I have rarely enjoyed working with someone as much. One day soon, when she is one of the biggest names in publishing, it will be my greatest literary claim to fame to say she taught me much of what I know.

My family: Liz, Sonam, Tashi, Jack, and future author Anna.

My late father, Kesang. If he was alive today he would have bought 8,000 copies of this book himself.

My darling wife, Samantha. It takes the acknowledgements section of a book for her to know that I love her because let's face it, I am better at watching cricket than I am at being romantic. Yet, without her I would be a different person, much less compassionate and slightly wealthier. All I want is for our kids to grow up to be like her.

My daughter Tara for being the most creative storyteller I know, and my mini-me son Jett, for waking me up so many times at night that all I can do is write.

I often wonder if my writing should pack more punch, but thanks to Sam, Tara and Jett, it suits me just fine to be an incredibly happy but confused author.